WHAT BLOOMS BENEATH

A.D. ELLIS

Gage-

*Thank you for believing in me and encouraging me
to continue writing this story even when I was convinced
it would never see the light of day.*

INTRODUCTION

A NOTE FROM THE AUTHOR BEFORE YOU BEGIN READING-

Rhône is a genderqueer, intersex individual who uses gender neutral pronouns in this story. Rhône prefers they/them and zie/zir. They/them and zie/zir are used interchangeably in this story. Zie replaces he/she and zir replaces him/her. The author links to more information on gender neutral pronouns later in this note.

A note on intersex:

Information about real-world intersex individuals can be found at The Intersex Society of North America. http://www.isna.org/faq/what_is_intersex

One of the fictional parts of this story and where the author took liberties is that Popids have completely functioning male and female sex organs and systems, and that they aren't subject to gender assignment surgeries as non-consenting infants and/or hormones trying to force their body to act a certain way.

Quoted from http://www.isna.org "The Intersex Society of North America (ISNA) is devoted to systemic change to end shame, secrecy, and unwanted genital surgeries for people born with an anatomy that someone decided is not standard for male or female.

We have learned from listening to individuals and families dealing with intersex that:

• Intersexuality is primarily a problem of stigma and trauma, not gender.

• Parents' distress must not be treated by surgery on the child.

• Professional mental health care is essential.

• Honest, complete disclosure is good medicine.

• All children should be assigned as boy or girl, without early surgery."

A note on intersectionality:

Kellan and Rhône (like so many of us) have a great deal of intersectionality.

**https://www.dictionary.com/browse/intersectionality

**https://www.ywboston.org/2017/03/what-is-intersectionality-and-what-does-it-have-to-do-with-me/

A note on gender neutral pronouns:

The author used they/them and zie/zir pronouns for

Rhône and other Popids. There are several other gender neutral pronouns. Read more here: https://uwm.edu/lgbtrc/support/gender-pronouns/

Also, the use of singular they is becoming (and should become) more used and accepted.

   **https://public.oed.com/blog/a-brief-history-of-singular-they/

   **https://www.grammarly.com/blog/use-the-singular-they/

   **https://aceseditors.org/news/2017/ap-style-for-first-time-allows-use-of-they-as-singular-pronoun/

A note on gender-related terms:

A glossary of gender-related terms-

   *https://www.hrc.org/resources/glossary-of-terms

   *https://www.glaad.org/reference/lgbtq

   *https://www.glaad.org/reference/transgender

Some other words it may be helpful to know:

• *Enby- In the LGBTQ community, an enby is a nonbinary person. It's a phonetic pronunciation of NB, short for nonbinary, or people who do not identify their gender as male or female.*

   • *Non-binary- An adjective describing a person who does not identify exclusively as a man or a woman. Non-binary people may identify as being both a man and a woman, somewhere in between, or as falling completely outside these* categories. While many also identify as transgender, not all non-binary people do.

• **Pansexual-** Describes someone who has the potential for emotional, romantic or sexual attraction to people of any gender though not necessarily simultaneously, in the same way or to the same degree.

• **Gender non-conforming** - A broad term referring to people who do not behave in a way that conforms to the traditional expectations of their gender, or whose gender expression does not fit neatly into a category.

• **Genderqueer** - Genderqueer people typically reject notions of static categories of gender and embrace a fluidity of gender identity and often, though not always, sexual orientation. People who identify as "genderqueer" may see themselves as being both male and female, neither male nor female or as falling completely outside these categories.

ONE

KELLAN ROBERTS

EARTH, the year 2044

"What is this place?" The words escaped, echoing in the damp cave before I could stop them.

The person in front of me stopped dead before turning. Dark eyes, wide and filled with fear, gazed in my direction.

"How did you f-find your way here? Y-you shouldn't be here."

"I followed you from the Department of Natural Resources Preservation." I shrugged. "You left your soil sample. I tried to catch up, but couldn't get your attention until you stopped here." I glanced behind me to the waterfall I'd slipped behind to follow the object of my pursuit. In front of me, to my left, a ray of sunlight filtered through the rock wall and illuminated a purple haze behind the...person? Creature? Being? I wasn't exactly sure. I wanted to say person; they looked very much like a human, but I couldn't be sure.

"Ah, yes, the sample. Um, well, thank you kindly. You may leave it there on that rock and be on your way."

He...? She...? Honestly, I wasn't sure. Nothing worse than misgendering a person. For the time being, I'd go with the gender-neutral they or them. *They* threw a furtive glance over their shoulder toward a dark opening in the cave wall, hidden slightly by a large rock, before flipping long blond hair from their eyes. A very pale and serious face glared at me as if willing me to leave.

"Wait, what's your name? What university do you attend?" I took a step forward and immediately a warmth consumed my body despite the cool dampness of the cave.

"University?" The head cocked. "I don't attend a university."

"Oh, my bad, I just assumed since you were bringing in soil samples that you were a student. I work there most days as a custodian." I stepped closer still and put out my hand. "I'm Kellan Roberts, by the way."

The person stared at my hand as if it were a snake preparing to strike. Several awkward moments passed before a hand reached out to tentatively touch mine. Even in the dim light of the cave, I could see pale, almost translucent skin, highlighted by a barely-there purple shimmer. A pleasant current skittered up my arm when our hands touched.

"I'm Rhône. Thank you for bringing me my bag, but I really must go." Rhône snatched the bag before scurrying behind an enormous rock and disappearing.

"Wait, don't go," I called out, but Rhône was gone.

———

FOR AN ENTIRE WEEK, I watched people coming and going at the Department of Natural Resources Preservation. I was a custodian with hopes of eventually taking enough classes and earning enough knowledge to be on staff, despite the government not usually allowing very many people to succeed in their choice of career. My real dream was to work in the Department of Paranormal, Supernatural, and Fantasy Sciences, but I'd failed every application I'd submitted. I simply had not an iota of paranormal, supernatural, or fantasy—*extra-sapien*—in my veins. Because the DNRP worked so closely with the DPSFS, I'd finally convinced myself that working with natural resources would be my next best bet.

For a week, I didn't see Rhône at the DNRP, which was frustrating.

But the frustration turned to confusion, intrigue, and anxious wonder when I retraced the steps I'd taken on the day I followed Rhône and found *not a single trace* of the waterfall, the cave, the rocks, absolutely *nothing*.

"Kellan, you clearly were trippin' on some good shit," Dayne, my ex-girlfriend but still somewhat close friend, stated when I shared the mystery.

Dayne and I had broken up for several reasons. First, she swore she wanted to "set me free" because of my pansexuality. I honestly think Dayne just wanted the freedom to sleep around without feeling guilty. I likely loved her at some point but Dayne getting arrested for breaking and entering at the Department of Paranormal, Supernatural, and Fantasy Sciences clenched our separation. The government prohibited college education and career advancement to felons or their significant others.

"See, me breaking up with you made things easier all around," Dayne was always saying.

It made no sense how our government could claim to be a democracy and boast freedom and equality for all while being filled with the most corrupt and dirty leaders known to man. My parents said that my birth in 2016 was right on the cusp of world corruption and iniquity, which then took a gigantic turn for the worse. Twenty-eight years later, that wicked unscrupulousness had only worsened. The government claimed not allowing felons or their significant others to further their education or careers was an important step in keeping a balance in society. I saw it as yet another way for the privileged—those with the advantage of money, race, class, and the *right* family—to further themselves from those with no privilege. I often questioned how our society had changed in such polar ways. My parents spoke of the slow, almost stealthy ways the corruption of government had begun. And I had witnessed that same, almost imperceptible, change in my lifetime. However, there had also been drastically quick changes. And all for the worst. I'd once come across a nearly sixty-year-old book titled *The Handmaid's Tale,* and the story very much reminded me of how the society of my birth had changed in such a terrifyingly swift and nefarious way. Many of the changes had taken place literally over night.

"I wasn't *trippin'* on anything, Dayne," I huffed. "I don't do anything except the government-approved natural mood and health enhancers." I ran a hand over my coarse, black hair. "I swear to you, that waterfall and cave and *person* were there."

Dayne chewed on a perfectly polished fingernail and shook her long blonde locks. "Kel, a waterfall and cave don't just appear and disappear. They just don't. Even if it was in an area you aren't super familiar with, natural landforms don't just show up one day and disappear the next." She stood and wrapped her arms around my waist. "You need to stop worrying about it. Maybe it was a dream. Maybe you got some bad pot. I know the government swears it's high quality, but you know there's still wacky weed out there. Come out with me and Steph; she's got a hot-as-sin brother, and you two would be absolutely beautiful together. He's super masc; no fem gay boys for you, right?"

Her cackle grated on my last nerve. Removing her arms from my waist, I stepped away. "Dayne, listen. I hate when you get all judgmental about people. For someone who supposedly 'loves all types,' you sure have a lot of types you don't like. I won't stand here and listen to you badmouth a feminine guy or a transgender person. I'm attracted to almost any person as long as they are good and kind." I held my hand up to stop her when she started to protest. "I don't want to come out with you and Steph. I don't want you fixing me up with guys you think are *right* for me." I glanced at my phone. "Look, I gotta go. I'll talk to you later." I left, probably rudely, but Dayne's judgement had pissed me off.

I was early for my shift, but the option of going home held no appeal. My meager paycheck barely covered rent on my shabby apartment, food, bills, and the occasional splurge on entertainment or clothing. The government provided all workers with uniforms, and I often found myself wearing khaki pants, a light blue button-up, and brown boots even off the clock. I wasn't living in poverty, but the government never really allowed anyone in my social class to thrive. Riches were saved for only the top echelon.

When I was a child, the country had divided— brutally and devastatingly for a large majority of the population. All businesses within the remaining region were government-run. States no longer existed. There was one government capital, and if you wanted any chance of surviving, let alone succeeding, you lived close to the government and worked for it in some way. Women and people of color were often allowed the same jobs as their white, male counterparts, but were paid less and expected to do more. It wasn't fair, but a job was a job; a job meant survival. Survival wasn't terribly difficult in the inner rings of the country, but succeeding beyond surviving didn't happen for most.

So, when I found myself at the government pavilion, I glanced around at the large, concrete, three-story buildings and let my heavy thoughts weigh on me. Department of Defense, Department of Food and Agriculture, Department of Medicinal Natural Drugs, Department of Finance...the names went on and on, and the buildings stretched out before me, and each one housed several divisions and subdivisions of their larger department.

The Department of Paranormal, Supernatural, and Fantasy Sciences had developed, as I'd learned from years of research, in a roundabout way. A few years before I was born, from what I could gather, a government employee had exploited friendly connections he had with some members of the magic, supernatural, and paranormal world. The fantasy, paranormal, supernatural worlds and all of the subsections of them had existed for all time, but few acknowledged it. However, when this government employee exposed some of the members, a small sector of the population—mostly dirty government officials—decided to use the magic, supernatural, and paranormal worlds for their own good. The Department of Paranormal, Supernatural, and Fantasy Sciences was set up, mostly in the beginning as a façade so that the government could control them. Of course, bad apples existed in all walks of life, and *some* members of the extra-sapien worlds allowed themselves to be used by the government. But the vast majority of these worlds worked for good and spent much of their time fighting off the government and their dirty ways. Researching this information hadn't been easy. Most of the mainstream publications would have a person believe that the government simply created DPSFS out of a progressive need to know more, to expand, to be more inclusive to all. But that was a load of bullshit. I found some articles, blogs, and anonymous interviews that told the real story of why DPSFS had come to be. And my parents and a few other older people had corroborated my research. I was glad DPSFS existed, and I felt such an incredible pull toward it, but I was also glad I knew the real reason *why* DPSFS had been created. It made me laugh to think that creating it had really backfired on the government, but they couldn't backpedal and take it away once they'd made such a grand statement about its creation.

By the time I reached my building, I had unknowingly made up my mind. I would request a meeting with Doctor Maeve Winston. Dr. Winston was the highest power in the Department of Paranormal, Supernatural, and Fantasy Sciences. If anyone would know about the disappearing waterfall and cave, it was her. The question was, would she see me? And if she did, would she be willing to share information with a mere commoner?

TWO

"AH, now just what do we have here?" A small-in-stature, plump character bustled into the office where I sat in a chair across from a large desk. Dr. Winston had a high raspy voice, a face set to serious, almost white hair which contrasted beautifully with her dark skin, and deep brown eyes which sparkled like diamonds. She reminded me of images I'd seen of fairy godmothers in childhood tales.

"Kellan Roberts, Dr. Winston. Thank you so much for seeing me on such short notice." I stood to shake her hand. I immediately knew I was in the presence of greatness. Her short stature by no means diminished her prominence.

She took my larger hand in her smaller, darker one. Maeve Winston hadn't aged since the first time I saw her when I was a small boy. As the top authority on all things extra-sapien, she likely had access to some of the most amazing anti-aging charms and spells along with contact with immortal souls. It shouldn't have been surprising she looked barely twenty-five when I *knew* she was *at least* sixty-seven, if not older.

"It's not polite to question an elder's age, and call me Maeve," she quipped, clearly reading my mind, as she squeezed my hand gently. She cocked her head to the side. "Kellan Roberts," she pondered while looking me up and down. "Ah, yes, tenacious and determined Kellan Roberts. Not a member of the paranormal, supernatural, or fantasy worlds, but definitely an ally. I've found your continued application to the DPSFS inspiring. It really is a shame you're not one of us." She tapped her chin. "What can I do for you today, Mr. Roberts?"

I shifted in my chair, suddenly nervous. Would she believe me? "Last week I followed someone. They had left their bag at the DNRP. I thought maybe it was an important soil sample."

Maeve listened, her face serene

"I followed them behind a waterfall," I continued, but I caught an almost imperceptible widening of Maeve's eyes. "When I caught up with them, they appeared to be getting ready to disappear behind a rock, maybe underground. That waterfall had never been there before and isn't there now."

"Go on," Maeve prodded, her fingers steepled under her chin.

"They seemed very spooked when I spoke. Like they

definitely didn't want me there. I was able to shake their hand and find out their name is Rhône."

"What else?" Maeve's gaze seemed to penetrate my soul.

"Rhône's skin was super pale, like translucent, kind of shimmery, sort of like a layer of sparkly powder." I pictured the day behind the waterfall, the sun filtering through the rocky cave wall. "Long pale hair, dark eyes, and there was a purple haze."

Maeve smiled softly and nodded. "Ah, yes, you've met a Popid villager."

It was my turn for wide eyes. "Popid villager? I'm sorry, I have no clue what that is."

She was silent for a long moment. "Sometimes the less you know, the better. Easier to protect the innocent that way."

"Please, I have no ill-intent. I'm just confused about how an entire waterfall and cave and person can be there one moment and gone the next."

"The fact that you saw them could mean you've got some sort of connection to the Popid village. Although, that would almost definitely require extra-sapien blood of some sort." Maeve frowned as she spoke. "The other option is that the village isn't thriving, possibly dying. And that would be catastrophic."

When I scrunched my face, Maeve continued, "The village's life source is the earth. When Earth suffers, the Popids suffer."

"Please, can you tell me about them?"

Maeve pursed her lips. "If I were to tell you about the Popids, you would be sworn to secrecy. You'd be responsible for their lives."

"I swear."

"Let me make it clear that I'm only sharing *any* information because you were able to follow Rhône behind the waterfall. That either means you possess something special or something is very wrong."

I leaned forward in my seat. "You have my word."

Maeve checked the time on the wall before pressing a button on her intercom. "Katarina, please hold my calls and move my meetings to tomorrow." Dr. Winston sat back in her chair as if to settle in for story time. "The Popid Village is hidden to the majority of Earth dwellers. The fact that you've seen it is baffling."

"So where is this village? How is it hidden?"

"The waterfall you saw hides a vast cave in which the villagers have lived for several generations, likely for many more decades than we're even aware. Possibly a century." Maeve leaned forward in her seat and propped her chin in a hand.

"But why did I see the waterfall one day, and now it's completely gone?"

Maeve held up a hand. "Patience. Please stop with the questions. I'll explain as much as I can."

"Sorry." I grimaced, and felt my cheeks heat.

"The Popid Village is an open, harmonious society

living with complete equality for all. Their members are gender nonbinary, gender nonconforming, and intersexual. They absorb their power from the purple popid flower, a cross between a poppy and an orchid. The popid flower's life source is the earth." Maeve gave a worried sigh. "The more the earth turns toxic and negative, the more the popid grows weak, which is why I'm concerned about the fact you were able to see the waterfall."

"Are they paranormal creatures? Supernatural? Witches?"

"The Popids have their own version of magic. When their magic is mixed with the purple haze of the popid flower, it's almost like a miracle grow potion. It keeps nature thriving; it keeps the village alive and well. There's no proof, since we can't study the Popid village very easily, but I have my theories that the muscovite also plays a part in the positivity of the Popids and the magic."

"Muscovite?"

"It's a mineral found in the cave. It makes the villagers' pale, almost translucent skin—which is mostly from living underground much of their lives— have a slight shimmery quality to it. I think it also increases their magic abilities." Maeve sat back in her seat.

Overwhelmed by Dr. Winston's information, I was quiet for a long moment. More than once, I started to ask a question, my mouth opening like a fish, but I couldn't even find the words to form a coherent question. "So, what do I do with this information?" I finally asked.

"My gut tells me to beg you to forget this information and what you saw," Maeve began, "but I can tell you're intrigued and likely won't listen. You *must not* allow anyone to follow you to the waterfall."

"But I thought you said it was hidden," I interrupted.

"It should be. It always has been, but as far as I can tell from your continued denied applications to DPSFS, you have no paranormal, supernatural, or magic blood, and yet you could see it." Maeve frowned and doodled with a pen. "Which means their charms and magic may be suffering or perhaps are being tampered with. The entire village, and maybe even the popid fields are withering. If anyone were to follow you, it could mean sure death to the entire Popid village. Unaccepting humans are a very dangerous thing for Popids."

"What if I see Rhône again?" My heart thumped as I recalled Rhône's long, pale hair, translucent, shimmery skin, and wide, dark eyes. I wanted to be close to him— her? —them? Dr. Winston had said gender nonbinary and nonconforming, so *them* seemed most accurate until I knew Rhône better. Why was I so drawn to them? Why did the image of them in that cave make my heart flutter?

"The villagers have interacted with Earth dwellers before, although I've never seen *true* friendships develop. That doesn't mean relationships *haven't* developed. I've just not had the opportunity to observe them in any positive or productive ways." Maeve's eyes stayed on the flower she was drawing. "The Popid village is self-sufficient; they don't *need* the outside dwellers."

"But you said their popid flower and their life source feeds upon the earth? If the earth is dying physically or socially, wouldn't that affect the villagers?" My heart inexplicably constricted for a population of people I'd never met and had no connection to.

Dr. Winston pursed her lips. "Well, yes, you are very right in that aspect. The villagers need the earth, but they don't *need* humans. However, they do *need* humans to keep the earth alive and well."

"And what a fucked-up job we're doing of that," I bit out. "Sorry."

"No need. You speak the truth." Maeve began doodling another flower. "I had such high hopes when new divisions of the government were created. We've made some great strides in so many ways, but our world is still filled with such hatred, such negativity. It's a toxic place, and Mother Earth cannot survive when surrounded by that."

"So, if I see Rhône, I can talk to them?" I hedged again.

"I'm quite pleased that you've adopted the enby pronouns for Rhône. You're well ahead of so many." Maeve cocked her head and studied me. "Such a shame that all the progress society had been making was wiped out by the government."

"Which is crap. Nonbinary, gender nonconforming, all of that has been around for *so long*. I don't get how there are *still* people who refuse to use a person's pronouns. And it *is* refusal. No one can claim they don't know; it's just plain old hatred and bigotry."

Maeve nodded. "I would agree. But when the government supports that hatred and bigotry, they make it impossible to escape."

"So, I *can* talk to Rhône?"

"There's that persistence."

I waited.

"May I ask why you're so insistent?"

I felt my cheeks heat, and I bit my lip. "Rhône was beautiful, mesmerizing, intriguing, and I want to know more about them."

Maeve was silent for several moments before speaking. "Certain organizations want to study and learn about the Popids, both the villagers and their flowers. Some of these organizations have only good intentions; they simply want to learn of the Popids' ways and their powers to try to use them in the outer world."

"But even that could cause harm to the Popids?"

"Yes, and sadly, more groups exist who outwardly express their fear and hatred toward the Popids, their existence as intersex, their ways—both in regards to their gender nonbinary and their magic—and want nothing more than to destroy them."

"Why?" My question came out harsher than I meant for it to be.

"Why do mere humans hate anything?"

"Fear of the unknown, fear of what they don't understand, the belief that different is scary and bad." I sighed. Our world was much further ahead of where it once was in regards to bigotry and racism and general prejudices, but we still had so damn far to go thanks to the setbacks our own government had supported over the last two decades.

"Exactly." Maeve tapped a finger on her bottom lip. "A friendship with Rhône isn't forbidden, but I worry about what vulnerabilities it could bring to the Popids."

"Maybe I'll never see the waterfall again. Maybe I'll never see Rhône again." My heart hurt at that thought. Rhône had somehow captured my attention and my heart within mere moments of meeting. "And if I do see them, our friendship could be only in the outer world. I don't ever have to go to the waterfall, even if I do see it again." I sat back in my chair and drew in a deep breath; my desperation was evident.

"Kellan, I can't tell you to never see Rhône. I can't tell you to never go to the waterfall or the cave; if you *do* see the waterfall again, only a villager can invite you into the cave." Maeve frowned. "See, this is where my worry comes in. In all of my time as director of DPSFS, the Popids have been completely protected. Their village was hidden, and only those with extra-sapien skills could feel, find, see the waterfall and hidden cave. Only a villager could invite outsiders in if it ever came to that. But now, a person with no apparent extra-sapien blood has seen the waterfall and ventured behind it. I'm worried others could do the same. The last line of defense is the invitation, but perhaps a person with ill-intent could overpower the Popid and gain access."

I wouldn't know why I was able to see the waterfall and cave until I could speak to Rhône; I moved onto a different question. "Do the Popid villagers or flowers help the earth in any way?"

"Yes, from what I've been able to gather from my studies and my seeing and empath skills. It is my firm belief that the Popid village, beings, and flowers bring a positivity to the earth. I, and other extra-sapien leaders, can feel the good, the change for the better from deep within Mother Earth. I theorize that the Popid beings have gatherings or ceremonies and that's when the outer world benefits from the positivity. The popid flowers are a salve for our dying natural world, a magic that counteracts earth's toxicity, and the negativity spewed by our dwellers."

"So, these groups intent on destroying the Popids, they need to understand that by destroying them, they are destroying Earth." I rubbed my palms on my jeans. "Why is that so hard for them to understand?"

"My dear child, these groups neither believe what they deem ramblings by a crazy old woman, nor do they care about the possibility of destroying our earth."

"You're the top expert of all things paranormal, supernatural, and fantasy! How can they not believe you?"

"The DPSFS is a division of the government that *many* don't believe in, even the majority of the government itself. We are whacks, cuckoos, witches, evil, the list goes on and on." Maeve sighed. "And in some ways, they are right."

"What?"

"Many fakes exist, trying to make a quick buck, which gives the true extra-sapien being a bad name. And yes, some *are* very evil, and the rest work constantly to keep good winning over evil, but some monsters get through the cracks. Not all of the paranormal, supernatural, fantasy world is good and kind, and it's hard to overcome our bad publicity. And who's to say what's *good* or *bad*. It's all somewhat relative."

I sat quietly for several moments, absorbing all I had learned.

"What other questions do you have, Kellan?"

I considered her question. "None right now. Or at least none I can put together in my head." I stood. "May

I contact you or come in if I have questions or run into trouble?"

"Yes, please." Maeve wrote a number on the back of a card. "This is my personal number. Contact me if you have even the slightest inkling something is wrong, for example if you believe others can see the waterfall, or *anything*."

"And if I see Rhône again?" I took the card and slid it into my back pocket.

"Tell them what you and I discussed. Maybe they are well aware of these possible breaches and issues in their village."

"Will do. Thank you, Dr. Winston." I shook her hand and turned to leave.

"Kellan?" Maeve called out.

I paused with my hand on the door and looked over my shoulder.

"One moment, please." She pulled out a piece of paper and wrote on it for several moments before folding it and slipping it into an envelope. Across the flap she signed her name with the date before sealing it. "Please sign this."

I raised a brow. "What is it?"

"Something I will share with you when this is all said and done. I want you to sign it today so you know it's the exact same letter if and when you ever get to read it."

Weird. "Sure." I penned my signature across the

envelope. "What do you mean 'when this is all said and done,'" I asked.

"My powers are telling me this is just the beginning and that you have an important part to play in how it all goes down."

She opened a safe on the wall and slipped the envelope inside.

THREE

"KELLAN, you got someone at the front desk asking for you," a fellow DNRP employee stuck his head into the supply closet where I was preparing the cleaning solution for mopping.

I found the process relaxing. I loved watching the water turn blue as the chemical was added. I shut off the water and scratched my head. "Who is it?"

He shrugged.

My parents and I were fairly close, but they wouldn't stop by for a visit. Dayne wasn't allowed in most government buildings. And I didn't have a lot of other friends. I nearly swallowed my tongue when I walked to the front desk and saw Rhône.

"Oh, hey, hi," I stuttered. "Rhône, hi." I walked around the counter and placed a hand on their shoulder. "Gosh, hi, it's good to see you."

Rhône smiled. Their eyes were hidden behind dark

sunglasses, and their skin, what I could see of it, appeared even paler with the same very slight purple hue and shimmer as at our last meeting. Rhône wore long sleeves and long pants, but the material was soft and light, not heavy like my work clothes. Their feet were covered in a soft leather wrap-around shoe the likes of which I'd never seen. Rhône's long, blond hair nearly sparkled under the fluorescent light, and I noticed the same soft leather around their feet was also woven into the thick braids they wore around their face.

"Are you able to speak? Possibly outside?" Rhône whispered.

"Oh, um, yeah. Sure." I glanced around for someone, anyone. "Just let me tell someone I'm taking a break." I caught the eye of another custodial staff member and pointed to my watch. When he nodded, I turned to Rhône. "I get fifteen minutes."

We left the building through a side door. Rhône immediately shielded their eyes and pointed to a covered table. "Can we sit in the shade? The heat and intensity of the sun are uncomfortable for my eyes and skin."

"I'm really glad you came to see me," I murmured as we sat under the shade, facing each other, knees touching. "But why did you come to see me?"

Rhône leaned forward and took my hand in theirs. "What did you see the day you followed me?"

Disappointment flooded my chest. I'd naively been hoping Rhône came to see me because they felt some sort of connection or draw to me like I was feeling to them.

Rhône squeezed my hand in encouragement.

"Um, a waterfall. A cave. A large rock wall."

"And have you seen the cave or waterfall since that day?"

I sighed and shook my head. "No, but not for lack of trying."

"I need your help. What time is your work day over?" Rhône leaned in closer and grasped my hands tighter.

"What? Oh, I'm off in"—I glanced at the large clock on the outside of the building—"two hours."

"I will be here, waiting, if that's okay."

"You can't sit here for two hours," I began.

"No, I'll take care of my errands and then come back."

"Okay, that's fine. I'll do my best to be out right on time." I cleared my throat. "Um, would you maybe like to grab dinner or something?"

Rhône smiled softly. "Help me first, and we'll go from there."

My heart thumped. "Yeah, okay, that sounds like a plan."

———

TWO HOURS LATER, I found Rhône at the same table.

The day had turned slightly cooler, and they wore a sweater of sorts.

"Hi." Rhône waved.

I smiled. "Hi." I'd never in my life had such an extreme and immediate draw, attraction, connection, *whatever this was* to someone. I fought the urge to pull them into my arms, to hold them, protect them, *love* them. Instead, I clenched my fists at my sides.

Rhône glanced at my hands and then to my face. Immediately, I calmed and relaxed my fists.

"We should go." Rhône stood and gestured for me to follow.

I fell into step beside Rhône. "What is it you need my help with?"

"Do you know anything about me? About my home? My people?"

"I spoke to Dr. Maeve Winston at Paranormal, Supernatural, and Fantasy Sciences. She told me quite a bit, or as much as she was comfortable or able."

"I apologize if this is a repeat," Rhône began. "I am a Popid. A member of the Popid village. Our people, almost a century ago, created the popid flower. It's a cross between an orchid and a poppy. The purple popid flower and our village gather strength of life from your earth. Our magic, our charms, our powers, they grow when Mother Earth is happy and peaceful. But our life source is slowly dying as Earth becomes more and more filled with hate, negativity, and toxicity." Rhône paused.

"Maeve did explain most of this," I shrugged. "Thank you for explaining though.

"What did she say about your ability to see the waterfall?"

"That I would either need to have extra-sapien blood, which she knows is not the case." I bit my lip before continuing, "Or that the Popids' powers are struggling, and the charm that hides the waterfall is slipping."

"Yes, that is our fear. There is even talk of a traitor amongst us." Rhône brushed a wisp of hair from their face. "But we are also highly interested in why *you* were able to see the waterfall when no one else saw it that day."

"Yeah, that's really weirding me out. I mean, it's a gigantic waterfall. No way others wouldn't have seen it."

"That's why we need your help." Rhône touched my arm softly, but removed their hand quickly when a zap of current shocked us. "I'm sorry, I should not have touched you without permission."

I smiled and held my hand out to Rhône. "It's okay. You have my permission. May I have yours?"

Rhône's face glowed and they reached for my hand. The current returned and immediately my blood warmed. Never had one hand in another looked so amazingly right and so perfect. I fought to draw my gaze away from our linked hands. Did they have some sort of power over me? Was I under a charm?

Rhône chuckled. "No, I have not charmed you."
They bumped a hip against mine. "I do have the power
to do that if I so choose, but this connection is all on its
own."

"Whoa, that's creepy."

"What? I can't always hear people's thoughts so
clearly, but yours are sparkling clear to me." Rhône
tapped the side of their head.

"So, you feel it too?"

"Yes, since that day in the cave. I've spoken to the
elders, and they are as perplexed as I am. I don't
understand the draw I feel toward you, just as I don't
understand your ability to see the waterfall and venture
behind it to view the cave."

"If helping your village means getting to spend time
with you, I'm in." I squeezed Rhône's hand gently.
"Plus, this is likely the closest I'll ever get to actual
work in the extra-sapien sciences," I added with a
shrug.

We arrived at the area I swore I'd seen the waterfall.
I glanced around and saw nothing even slightly
resembling a waterfall. Trees lined the park's paths
along with benches, picnic areas, and a very large
playground. But definitely no waterfall.

"It's not here." My shoulders slumped.

"Good, we've increased our charm to keep it
hidden." Rhône dropped my hand. "I'll speak to the
elders first. Then we'll do some experimenting. Stay
here, I'll be back."

Rhône walked away and simply disappeared—disintegrated? —into thin air.

"Holy hell," I whispered and looked around to see if anyone had noticed. Several people were on the sidewalks, playing at a nearby playground, a couple were having a picnic, yet no one seemed to have seen a person just disappear. Were the people too busy? Too involved in their own thoughts? Why could *I* see Rhône walk into nothingness?

Several moments later, Rhône returned. "Okay, are you ready?"

"Can other people see you?" I blurted.

"Most appear to be able to see me." Rhône nodded.

"How do they not see you just disappear when you go walking into the village?"

"When the charm is working well, no one should notice it." Rhône pulled out a phone.

"You have phones?"

"Kellan, it's 2044, of course we have phones." Rhône waved the tiny device at me. "We even have the newest and best phones."

"Hmmm, I guess that makes sense. Your people created a whole new flower, have magic charms, and get your power from the earth." I smiled wryly. "Phones don't seem too strange when you think of it that way."

"So, I'm strange to you?" Rhône lifted an eyebrow.

"No, no, that's not what I meant." I reached for their hand. "This is just a lot to take in. A hidden world, a hidden people, magic? Just new to me, different. But not a bad strange or bad different. Just the opposite in fact, a good strange, a *good* different."

Rhône smiled. "I'm used to the outside world judging me. All of my people are. In the village, we don't have gender binaries. Popids are just beings. We have no gender constraints pigeonholing us to your male or female. In our village, we have the freedom to identify and present ourselves as masculine, feminine, or neutral as we choose. A large number of villagers choose gender neutral. We find that Earth dwellers put too much importance on specifying a gender, labeling it, and defining it."

"That sounds amazing." I ran a hand over my hair. "My parents tell about times before I was born, and for the first few years of my life; according to them, society was making a lot of progress with inclusion and accepting *all* people." I paused then frowned. "But I guess the government went from bad to worse and put a stop to any progress. Dad said it was like taking a thousand steps back and all the hard work toward acceptance was erased and inclusion was basically outlawed." I sighed. "Your world, *village,* sounds wonderful. Tell me more about it."

Rhône cocked their head to the side. "What would you like to know?"

"Are you the only Popids in the world?"

"No, several underground villages exist around the world. There are also some in different dimensions," Rhône explained. "What else?"

"So, no *him, he* or *her, she* pronouns?"

"No. All Popid beings are completely intersex and aren't labeled by the outer world's binary terms. Although some villagers *choose* to use outer world pronouns and have opted for male or female labels. Most who want to use outer world pronouns choose *they*. But many Popids have no pronouns, or they've created their own. Also, without having defined gender binaries, Popids are able to just exist. Some lean more toward what your world would describe as *male*. Some lean more toward your definition of *female*. Many are, to use your world's terms, multigender, genderqueer, agender...the list goes on and on because gender is not something Popids are overly caught up on."

"What *are* Popids caught up on?" I asked. "Oh, and I've been using *they* and *them* for you. Is that okay?"

"I'm open to those pronouns in the outer world. In the village, you may hear my pronouns as *zie* or *zir* or simply no pronouns at all." Rhône stopped for a moment before answering my next question. "Popids believe in a higher power, a power which created us as perfectly intersex and nonbinary. We believe it is our life's mission to be open and kind, to show love to each other, and to live peacefully while accepting and celebrating differences." Rhône paused to push the sunglasses up their nose.

"So, the village is just happy and peaceful and accepting of all?" It sounded so wonderful.

"Yes, our powers are the strongest when we work

together in peace and harmony. Everyone in the village has a position, a task to do, or a *job,* as you'd call it. We worship Mother Earth. We trade goods and services. The Popid village is nothing like your world." Rhône hung their head.

"Yeah, Earth is pretty screwed up." I sighed. "So, um, what do you do for fun?"

"We gather weekly, sometimes more often, for singing and dancing and sending positivity to our Mother Earth. The more good we can put into the universe, the more powerful we become. Plus, it brings us pleasure and enjoyment." Rhône twisted a braid.

"What about, um," I stuttered. "Reproduction. How do your people continue? Like babies and such."

A smile as bright as the sun lit Rhône's face. "Any individual can choose to reproduce if they would like. Our bodies have the ability to impregnate another, as well as carry a child and give birth. I believe the method is very similar to the reproduction of humans." They, *zie,* winked, and I felt my face flush.

"Sorry, I feel stupid about all of this."

"Don't." Rhône touched my face. "Your questions are understandable, and I feel comfortable answering them. You're not like others who question out of judgement or hatred."

"Do some of the Popids have breasts for feeding a baby? Or do you do it another way?" Lord, my face was so hot.

"A body that has carried a child and birthed that

child will develop the ability to feed the infant. We also have other methods of providing the baby's nourishment. But just like Earth dwellers, we have a variety of bodies. Some of us are tall; some are short. Some are thin; some are rounder. Some have more pronounced breasts, some like myself have nearly flat chests; and some choose to display their breasts while others choose to wrap them. We are intersexual so we have both sex organs, both outside and inside, meaning both a penis and a vaginal opening. Some Popids have large"—Rhône cleared their throat—"*cocks*, I believe is the word you would use, and some are small or almost nonexistent. And all of this is perfectly fine. No one is judged for their body or how they choose to present their body. No one is judged for the way in which they identify or the type of sex they choose to have or not have." Rhône glanced at the phone in their hand. "We have time for one more question."

I bit my lip so hard I tasted blood. "Is sex something your people do only for reproduction?"

Rhône's smiled broadened, and they leaned close. "Oh no, sex is much more for love and recreation than for reproduction. My people have no shame about sex. We celebrate our bodies and the pleasures we can find with ourselves and others."

"Oh," I breathed the word and felt like a total perv as my cock grew hard. Could Popids have sex with humans? Oh my God, I wanted to ask, but I didn't know how. I mean, I'd sound like a total ass to ask that.

But oh, how I wanted Rhône's body. Wanted to touch them, taste them, tease them, and pleasure them.

Rhône blushed and cleared *zir* throat. "Popids *can* have sex with humans. It's not something that happens often, but it's certainly not *prohibited*. There are records of past and more recent instances of Popids and humans procreating and that child is always welcome in the village if they so choose. Now, no more questions until later."

"Oh my God," I groaned and held my face in my hands. "I'm sorry, I forgot." Rhône's ability to hear my thoughts was...well, embarrassing.

"Don't feel embarrassed, Kellan." Rhône touched my face again. "Your desires match mine."

———

I SPENT the next couple hours telling Rhône when I could hear or see the waterfall. When it was somewhat visible, and when it was completely hidden. Rhône communicated with the village through their phone. Their serious expression relayed their concern about the safety of the village, but zie also beamed at me throughout the two hours and whispered, "There is something very special within you, Kellan. Don't ever doubt that."

Later, when Rhône invited me to the village, I couldn't see the waterfall, and my heart fell because the charm was working. "I can't see it right now," I muttered. "I mean, that's good, right? The village is safe." But I wasn't ready for my time with Rhône to end, and I very much wanted to see the Popid village.

"Silly, I can lead you to it." Rhône took my hand, and my blood zinged.

As I walked toward where the waterfall would be, I thought of something. "You speak very fluent English, although I hear a hint of an accent. Is English the language of the Popids?"

"Popids are fluent in many of the world's languages, but, yes, we have our own language."

Rhône looked at me as zie pulled me through a cool mist. I immediately recognized we were behind the waterfall. "Whoa, that's wild," I breathed. "The language thing and the fact that you basically just transported me."

"You will hear bits and pieces of many languages in the village. I'm one of several fluent in English which is why I'm often sent on errands." Rhône smiled. "Plus, I enjoy—or can endure better—most interactions with Earth dwellers while many of the other villagers don't."

"Why?" I asked, but I had a feeling I knew the answer.

"Not all outsiders are as friendly and accepting as you, Kellan." Rhône's smile fell, and sadness shadowed zir face. "Most are not."

Anger spread through me. When would our world learn to accept and celebrate differences rather than judging and hurting? Why did it seem like our history was filled with small steps forward and huge steps backward?

"You are possibly the first human to be *invited* into our village in several generations. Many human and Popid interactions take place in the outer world. Expect many curious eyes on you."

"What? Why?"

"My ancestors tried to invite Earth dwellers to learn of our ways, but too often hatred and negativity and harmful curiosity came with those invited, so we haven't invited outsiders in much. More than once, outsiders have attempted to bribe or forcibly remove Popids from the village in order to sell them to the highest bidder. Science, museums, freakshows, and the like." Rhône brushed a braid over their shoulder. "For some of the villagers, you may be the first outsider they've ever seen."

"Wow, that's kinda...overwhelming," I murmured.

"Tell me about what you're feeling."

"I guess it's just a lot at once. I'm learning of this hidden place, a place that sounds like somewhere so much better than where I live. I find out that for some reason I can see this place when others can't. I don't want to offend anyone if I don't use pronouns correctly. What if I'm a major disappointment? Like some have never seen an outsider, what if I'm not what they were expecting?" I drew in a deep breath.

"Kellan, my parents are lead elders of the village," Rhône began.

"That doesn't make me feel any better," I interrupted.

Rhône laughed. "My point is that I'm a trusted member of the village. All are trusted, but my instinct and intuition and powers are held in high regard. If I say you are an amazing person in possession of something special, and are to be trusted and respected and listened to, then the village takes my every word to heart. Me coming to find you, to ask for your help, inviting you behind the waterfall, all of those things speak of my extreme regard for your heart, your powers, and your support."

Their words floored me. "Rhône, I have no powers. I am nothing special. I work as a custodian at the Department of Natural Resources Preservation because it's as close as I'll ever get to DPSFS. I like to think I'm a good person, but beyond that, I'm nothing…"

Rhône's fingers touched my lips to stop my words. "I forbid you to say such things ever again. You may not have extra-sapien blood—although, a very large part of me questions the accuracy of that—but you definitely have something special or else you wouldn't be able to see the waterfall when others can't. I'm not saying you're the *only* one who can see it. I know many others in the extra-sapien community can see it—whether they are good or bad—which is why it's so important to get the charm strengthened and keep it working." Rhône tapped my lips. "You. Are. Special. And I *do* have powers, so you have to trust me."

I could only nod.

"There's one other thing."

"What? Do I need to be blindfolded? You'll have to erase my memory after I see the village?"

"You've watched too many movies." Rhône laughed. "Although, we *do* have the power to erase memories if needed. No, I *may* have let the village know that I've claimed you as mine."

I gulped and attempted to breathe. "Cool, cool...um, what does that mean exactly?"

Rhône chuckled. "Just a way to let others know that you're with me and not available to them. You are one of the most attractive people I've ever seen, and I know the village will be aflutter when they see you. I want them to know you're mine." Rhône's shoulders drooped. "I'm sorry, I realize now how terrible I was to do that. Perhaps you'll find a villager you're attracted to and want to spend time with them. I should not have..."

Their words eventually filtrated my brain, and I shushed them. "Rhône, stop." I placed my hands on their shoulders. "My attraction and interest in any Popid are *only* for you. My heart feels complete when I'm with you, and I want to spend time with only you."

"I have two questions," Rhône whispered.

I waited.

"One, I'm intersex, *and* my gender is very fluid. Are you open to a relationship with a genderqueer being?

Someone whose body is so very similar to yours, yet so very different?" Rhône lifted zir face to meet my gaze.

I choked on a laugh. "This is so bizarre, but so amazing. First, I think the question should be if I'm open to a relationship with a being from a hidden, magical world. That answer would be *yes*. As far as your gender, even if I didn't know anything about you, I'm insanely attracted to you despite your gender or lack thereof. I'm completely open to a relationship with a genderqueer person, especially if that person is you. Nothing about you being intersex bothers me; your body is beautiful. Always."

Rhône stepped closer. "Second question."

My breath caught.

"May I kiss you?"

"Oh, hell yeah," I murmured before dipping my head and allowing my lips to meet Rhône's.

The purple haze of the cave seemed to swirl and elevate us as a pleasant electric current traveled between our lips and through our bodies. I pulled Rhône closer, their arms wrapping around my waist and our hips meeting. My dick took an immediate interest in the solid mass bumping into me from behind Rhône's soft pants. Without thought, I shuffled toward the cave wall and pressed Rhône gently against the rock. They anchored their arms around my neck and lifted their legs to tangle around my hips. Rhône's body thrust and rocked and rode mine while never missing a beat in the kiss. Their hands ran along my head, fingernails gently scratching my scalp before breaking the kiss.

"I've never kissed an outsider, but that's the only kiss to ever take my breath away completely and cause such an immediate arousal." Rhône's words were gruff.

"I've never kissed a Popid, but no kiss has ever been so intimate and intense." I kissed them again and rocked our bodies together, finding pleasure in the catch of Rhône's breath. "But I definitely want to do it again." I kissed Rhône again. "And again." Another kiss. "And again."

"Agreed." Rhône rubbed their heated core into my cock. "But for now, I think we should meet the village."

Reluctantly, I let Rhône go. My heart thrilled when they took my hand and led me to the large rock at the back of the cave.

"It will be darker than you're used to. Your eyes will take a while to adjust. We do have lighting, but it's not the type you're accustomed to." Rhône took the lead down a long, damp, winding stone stairway.

With my heart pounding, my cock throbbing, and my hand held by the only person I ever wanted to spend time with again, I journeyed deep into the earth to discover a whole new world.

FOUR

"TURN on more of the lanterns, please," Rhône directed.

I let my eyes adjust to the darkness and could see shadowy figures of villagers. As more light filled the darkness, I was able to see the others more clearly. Rhône's description was spot-on; the Popids were of various shapes and sizes. Some had longer hair than Rhône; some had their hair cut shorter than my own. I saw beings presenting very masculine, some extremely feminine, but the vast majority appeared to be very gender neutral.

And all eyes were on me.

I gave a small wave and smiled.

"This is Kellan." Rhône gripped my hand. "He's been instrumental in helping with our security issue. He works for the Department of Natural Resources Preservation and is a trusted friend."

The villagers murmured quiet greetings.

"Would you like a tour?" Rhône asked.

"Very much, yes."

Rhône showed me the cave's inner parts where there was the largest kitchen I'd ever seen, an infirmary, an indoor training facility, and a dining room large enough to seat the entire village if needed. The living quarters were a combination of open concept, communal living as well as separate rooms with doors for more privacy.

"Most Popids choose to sleep in the communal area much of the time, but the private rooms are definitely used and appreciated by many at various times. Intimacy or just needing time to one's self." Rhône gestured to the private rooms. "My room and the rooms of the elders are separate from this area. But we often find ourselves gathering with the village for communal fellowship and comfort."

The inner workings of the cave seemed to stretch on forever. Laboratories, meditation rooms, rooms for creating and practicing spells, charms, wards, and the like, plus an entire school-like area, and a nursery for the youngest of the Popids.

"Although, most Popid parents keep their children with them at all times, it's recommended that the children attend the nursery and school to increase their social interaction with peers."

I nodded at Rhône's explanation as I took in all that the cave contained.

Throughout our tour, I noticed that the rock wall to my left was sometimes closed off to the outside and sometimes completely open. "So, there's more to the village out there?" I pointed toward one of the openings.

"Yes, we can go see the outer area."

Popid fields spread before us as far as my eyes could see. The plant stems were green, and the leaves were highlighted by the bright purple of the popid flower. I'd once seen an old digital clip of a golden wheat field waving in the breeze. This popid field reminded me of that field, but the waves of purple were even more gorgeous and mesmerizing.

We toured the outdoor training and recreation areas, the sacred areas used for gatherings and offerings to Mother Earth, and the gardens. Along with the popid fields, which took an entire team of intricately trained individuals to care for, the village had massive vegetable gardens along with flowering plant gardens.

"How do all of these plants grow underground?"

Rhône smiled and pointed overhead. "We've charmed openings to let in sunlight and rain. We collect both for use on our gardens and fields as needed. Much of our machinery and appliances are run by the solar energy we collect from the outer world. We have a water reclamation process one hundred times more effective than your world's. Much of the water used in our village has been used and recycled for generations. However, we *do* continue to collect fresh rainwater from the outer world. It takes us a very long time to clean the *fresh* water of all the chemicals it contains."

"So, the Popids have basically perfected solar energy and the water cycle?"

Rhône shrugged. "You could say that."

"It's too bad the outer world can't admit they could learn so very much from your village if they would just treat you with dignity and respect and stop acting like you're a bunch of freaks who need studied or exploited or destroyed." My anger at *my people*, if I even wanted to lower myself to claim them, was overflowing.

Rhône shrugged again. "Unfortunately, the outer world doesn't have the same open-minded attitude as you."

We arrived at a somewhat hilly area of the cave. "I can't believe an underground cave has rolling hills of grass. This is absolutely gorgeous."

"The hills are natural. The grass took some time to magic into growing even with the collected sunlight and rain. But it's taken hold and allows for the animals to graze."

My eyebrows flew up. "Animals?"

Rhône pointed.

I recognized chickens, cows, goats, and sheep. "Oh, wow! We don't even have ready access to these animals topside. Everything is manufactured and chemically produced. I've only seen some of these creatures in old books. Any *fresh meat* available in my world comes at a fairly steep price because it's so hard to come by."

"Our animals are not used for meat, only for their milk, eggs, and wool," Rhône quickly assured. "We don't often have fresh meat in the village. But a couple times a year we will work out a trade with outer worlders."

"So, one hundred percent fresh eggs and milk are used here in the village. You also make cheese? Butter?"

"Yes, we have many varieties of some of the most delicious cheeses. And cream, sometimes yogurt, and ice cream as a treat. Our sweet cream butter is better than anything you've ever tasted, I guarantee it. We also use the wool for much of our clothing and blankets."

I could only shake my head in wonderment.

An hour later, we found ourselves back at the expansive popid fields, and I was still fighting to pick my jaw up from the ground. "This village is completely self-sustained. You could live here for the rest of your life and *never* need to venture into the outside world."

Rhône nodded. "Yes, that's accurate."

"Truly amazing."

"We would have to give up some of the luxuries we've grown accustomed to," Rhône offered and waved their phone at me. "We take advantage and enjoy many of the outer world's creature comforts, but we aren't reliant on them. We don't *need* them. We can create anything a Popid might need, either through our skills or our magic."

My eyes were heavy and my heart full. "These are

one of the most gorgeous, mesmerizing flowers I've ever seen," I breathed.

"That's the power of the popids," Rhône teased. "It's an amazing flower, but you're definitely feeling the effects of its magic."

My body warmed and I wanted to dive into the field of purple flowers and make popid angels and frolic and stay there forever.

"Come on, the popids have a tight hold on you." Rhône took my hand. "I know I said we could possibly go out to eat, but I'd like you to meet the elders, and they'd very much enjoy if you stayed for dinner."

I could only smile and nod as Rhône pulled me away from the popids.

We came to a dining area of sorts deep inside the cave.

"Does the entire village eat together every night?"

"Oh no," Rhône stated. "The elders meet over dinner a couple times a week."

"And this is their normal night to gather?"

Rhône bit their lip. "Not exactly. They decided to meet for dinner so they could ask you to come, as well. They are curious. Some are suspicious. Some feel protective."

"So, I'm like meeting a table full of uncles and fathers? Great."

"Or aunts and mothers," Rhône teased and bumped my hip.

"Right, sorry," I stammered.

A group of ten people walked into the dining area. My pulse pounded, but at the same time my mind was at peace

"Hello, Kellan," the person in the middle greeted. "Please, let's all sit. Dinner is about to be served."

"Servants?" I whispered.

"No, villagers who enjoy cooking take turns preparing and serving meals."

The meal was delicious and a very happy occasion. The elders were polite, funny, and welcoming. I got the hint they'd done some research on me because they knew quite a bit. But it was understandable. They were allowing an outsider into their world and would want to have some background information.

"What questions do you have for us?" Nayel, one of Rhône's parents, asked from their position next to their spouse, Rube.

"I don't need a full-blown history or science lesson, but how did your people come to be?"

Rube fielded my question. "The Popids hold tight to the belief we were created by a higher being. Our bodies have been perfectly intersex since our creation. While intersex individuals in your outer world have often faced surgeries as nonconsenting infants, hormones trying to force the body to act a certain way, ridicule, secrecy, and shame, the Popids have bodies with both—as you would recognize, *male* and *female*—sex organs. A Popid, without getting into a detailed genetics discussion, has a mosaic of X and Y chromosomes resulting in our purposeful, normal, and accepted intersex features."

"Normal and accepted in the Popid village, but not so much in the still-very-unaccepting outer world?" I frowned.

"Sadly, yes. We stay hidden for several reasons and that's definitely one of them." Rube nodded.

"Some of the language I've heard sounds very fluent, even some outer world slang. Do Popids study language? How is the slang learned?"

Rube laughed. "Many of our villagers learn their multiple languages by being out in the outer world. So many of us can blend in fairly easily. We pick up languages, nuances, slang very quickly. Others immerse themselves in television and movies in certain languages. While we don't *need* the creature comforts of the outer world, we are not against taking advantage of them to increase our learning."

"A lot of the slang is learned by one or two and then passed along to others within the village," Rhône offered.

"Any other questions?" Nayel asked.

"How does one become an elder of the Popids?"

"The village nominates those they think would be best. If nominated, a Popid can accept the nomination or reject it. If they choose to run for elder council, they are asked to tell of their qualifications, their past, and their reason for wanting to be on the board," Nayel explained.

"Being an elder is an honor, but not for everyone," Rube added.

"Yes, Rube is correct, eldership comes with great responsibility. An entire village of Popids trusts and relies on us for their safety and continued well-being." Nayel took Rube's hand and kissed it.

"This is the most amazing place I've ever seen, I'm absolutely in love with it," I rambled. "I've never seen such beauty, felt such a welcoming atmosphere, and been at such peace in a new place. And I swear that's not just the popids talking."

Everyone seated at the table laughed.

"You come to us with high praise from Rhône, and after meeting you, I can see why." Rube smiled broadly. "I know it's still unclear exactly *what* you have, but you possess something special. Perhaps several special somethings."

I shrugged. "Thank you, but I don't know what it would be. I'm simply a custodian at the DNRP whose dream is to be part of the Department of Paranormal, Supernatural, and Fantasy Sciences. I work hard, I treat people kindly, and I stay out of trouble."

Nayel leaned forward and whispered theatrically, "When Rhône and Rube and a table full of elders say you're something special, don't argue. Just smile and say thank you."

I smiled and said, "Thank you."

By the end of the evening, I felt like a little kid who didn't want to leave his grandparents' house at the holidays. The Popids were so caring and kind and open and welcoming, and I never wanted to leave.

"We can come back," Rhône whispered, "but I'd like to see your place and spend time with you outside of my home."

Leaving wasn't such a terrible idea.

We said our goodbyes, and I breathed a sigh of relief when Nayel and Rube asked me to please return. "I'm not sure you could keep me away."

Nayel raised their eyebrows.

"Oh, well, I mean I guess you *could* keep me out. Charms and magic and powers and all," I stammered.

Nayel and Rube smiled.

"But I'm something special, so maybe not," I joked, having never been as comfortable around a group of people as I was with these villagers.

Everyone laughed, and I took Rhône's hand to head up the stone stairs as if it was something we'd been doing every night of our lives. My heart begged for it to be something we did for every night of our lives from that point on. "Is this real? This feeling? This connection? It's not magic or a charm or the popids?"

Rhône smiled softly and kissed my cheek. "It's real. Popids don't make a habit of controlling people with our powers. If you weren't feeling the same connection as me, I wouldn't power you into feeling it. It's the same as when Popids encounter Earth dwellers. We *could* use our magic to make them accept us, stop their hateful words, but we choose not to use our powers that way."

"I really don't understand what anyone could see in you to evoke their hatred. You're so very beautiful, all the Popids are, and you look so very human-like it's near impossible for anyone to know you're extra-sapien."

"When outsiders can't immediately determine if we fit their binary description of male or female, the hatred begins and grows."

"What utter bullshit," I growled.

"No more negative talk for now, I want our time together to be happy."

———

"SO, this is my place, not very impressive." I swept my hand to indicate my small apartment.

Rhône tugged on my shoulder to spin me around. "It's beautiful because it's your home. I feel you here, your essence." They kissed me, softly, and whispered, "Thank you for sharing this part of yourself with me."

"Just a tiny little apartment," I murmured against zir lips, loving the way my whole body came alive when we touched.

"Homes are very personal. You say this place isn't much, but it's where you eat, sleep, and rest." Rhône kissed me again and took my hand. "Show me around."

I chuckled because there was very little to show, but

I humored them and gestured around my little place. "Kitchen and nook. I don't have top-of-the-line appliances, but I think the items I have are better than the ones I've read about from the past. At least my kettle, stove, and toaster work quicker and more efficiently than in my parents' time." I turned and pointed out the other areas of my home. "My little bit of a bedroom, living area, and bathroom right there through the door."

"Are these your parents?" Rhône asked when they saw photographs in the living area.

"Yes."

"Are you close?"

"Fairly so. I mean, we don't see each other daily, because they're busy with work. But we see each other often enough and keep in touch."

"Do you have siblings?"

"No, just me."

"Tell me more about yourself." Rhône wandered to the couch and sat, patting the seat next to them.

I smiled and sat with them, both of us turned to face each other. "What would you like to know?"

"What were you like as a child?"

I thought for a moment. "Good kid. Followed the rules, treated people kindly, made good grades."

Rhône smiled. "I can see that."

"I became obsessed with all things paranormal, supernatural, and fantasy when I was about ten and declared I *would* work for them one day. I want to further my education and work for DPSFS, but I've applied year after year, and I get turned down every time." I frowned. "No extra-sapien blood."

Rhône scoffed. "I'm still not sure I believe that." They scooted closer to me, tangling our legs together on the couch. "Their loss if they don't accept you."

"Tell me something about your childhood."

Rhône tapped their lip.

"Oh, shoot, Popids *are* babies, right? I mean, I saw younger Popids in the cave. Do they start as babies?" I rambled. Slapping a hand to my face, I sighed. "Sorry, I'm nervous. I saw the nursery and your parents already told me some of this. I should just stop talking."

Rhône chuckled. "We are born the same as Earth dwellers. Our gestation ranges from six to twelve months depending on what the individual baby needs, but everything else is similar."

I nodded.

"I was a precocious child. My abilities were seen much sooner than others my age. And my powers were stronger. I quickly learned the enchantments, charms, and spells and then went on to create many of my own. Some I shared with the village; some I kept to myself."

I couldn't help but smile. "I can totally see you as the brilliant little one, always learning, maybe causing mischief."

"Yes, that was definitely me. I never caused problems or harm, but I was forever getting into things and experimenting." Rhône stroked my cheek. "I honed my basic skills early on and have been enhancing and exploring my powers ever since."

"Do you ever use your powers for evil," I teased and lightly tickled Rhône's arm, "or only for good?"

"Almost always for good," Rhône leaned in and kissed my neck, "but I assure you my evil is very, *very* good."

The blood in my veins immediately flowed like lava, my cock hardening.

"I'd like permission to explore your body," Rhône stated.

"You've got it."

"Say it," they demanded.

"You have permission to touch me, explore my body, whatever you want," I panted.

Rhône gripped my chin and made me look at them. "You may explore my body, touch me, and find pleasure in me."

They unbuttoned my shirt, slipping it from my shoulders and removing it from my body before their hands caressed my torso.

I grasped the hem of Rhône's shirt and tugged until it was over their head and joined mine on the floor. My hands roamed from Rhône's waist to their taut nipples before I wrapped my arms around their shoulders and pulled them close to ravish their mouth. There had to be magic in zir lips as I'd never been so turned on in my life.

"I'm not using magic on you," Rhône whispered

against my lips. "This is just what it feels like when two bodies are attracted at a spiritual and physical level." They broke from my mouth to trail kisses down my neck until they reached my nipples.

"Ahhh," I cried as if they had touched me with an electrical wire rather than just their tongue.

"Mmmm, so sensitive," Rhône purred and lapped at my nipples again. "Would you like to share orgasms?"

I laughed.

"What?"

"Sharing orgasms just sounds a little weird." I ran my fingertips softly down their back.

"Ah, yes, the slang." Rhône's tone became mockingly serious. "Jack off, finger me, jerk off, bust a nut, come, are those better?"

"Where did you learn those terms?"

"Earth-dweller pornography is quite educational and entertaining," Rhône quipped.

We both snorted in laughter.

"I say less talking and more doing," I growled and picked them up. Once at the bed, I hesitated. "Is this okay?"

"We are consenting adults with perfectly beautiful and healthy bodies. It's more than okay," Rhône breathed heavily against my chest.

I laid them down on the bed. "What do you want?"

"I want to"—Rhône paused as if considering their words—"suck your cock."

I groaned and palmed my raging erection. "What would you like me to do?"

Rhône slipped their pants off, uncovering an impressive package encased in a soft, loose boxer brief type design.

My mouth watered.

"I'd like you to suck me, touch me, taste me, and make me come."

"I can totally get behind that," I murmured as I stripped my pants and underwear, feeling my dick spring up to slap my belly.

Rhône shimmied out of their shorts, revealing a throbbing cock. They reached for me, and I joined them on the bed.

"Touch me, Kellan."

I gripped their length and stroked the heated skin. "Holy hell, that's gorgeous," I exclaimed as I jacked them with my fist.

Rhône bit zir lip, slid a hand between their legs, and moaned. "Suck me," zie demanded.

Continuing to stroke them, I bent to take the glistening cock deep into my mouth. From the first salty taste, to the stretch of my lips around their flesh, to the gagging sensation, I knew this person was exactly what I'd been missing my entire life.

Rhône's hand, slick with their own wetness, reached to grip my dick, and I nearly came apart.

"Oh, fuck. Shit, that's so good," I mumbled around their length.

"Make me come, Kel," Rhône commanded.

I sucked and tongued while my hand slipped to finger their hot, wet core. My slick finger trailed to Rhône's ass. "Is this okay?"

Rhône nodded and whimpered as they continued to stroke my cock.

I fingered Rhône's hole, teasing and testing. "You're tight."

"I want you to stretch me, open me up, and invade my body," Rhône panted. "But not tonight." They shifted to their back and took me between their legs. "Rub against me."

I rocked my hips, my cock thrusting against Rhône's.

They reached between our bodies and jacked our cocks in one hand while teasing my nipple with the other.

"Find your release, Kellan. Spill your seed." Rhône gasped as my dick erupted, and their own come mixed with mine.

Several moments later, sticky with our spunk, we lay catching our breaths.

"Did you find that enjoyable?" Rhône asked.

"Are you kidding me? That was the best sex I've *ever* had."

"And you were comfortable with my body being different than yours?"

I propped myself on an elbow. "Your body is different, but also very much the same. I didn't see it as anything but a beautiful body I want to be with. I loved every second of what we did and can't wait for more." I stopped myself from the one question on my mind.

"Go ahead, ask it."

I rolled my eyes and sighed. "No secrets with you, huh?'

Rhône shook their head.

"Do you prefer one type of sex over the other?" I felt my cheeks heat.

"It depends on my partner and the mood I'm in. I mostly enjoy anal, but I find pleasure in vaginal penetration as well."

I nodded. "Okay, good to know."

"I also enjoy," Rhône paused, "as outsiders call it, *topping*. Is that something that you find pleasure in?"

I swallowed. Hard.

"You mean for me to bottom? To be honest, I'm not sure. I've never been the bottom in a sexual relationship." I swallowed again and allowed myself to imagine taking Rhône's dick deep inside my ass. "But I'm definitely not ruling it out. Not in the slightest. I'm not sure I would have ever wanted that with someone else, but with you, I find myself wanting it all." I leaned in and kissed them. "Are you *sure* you've not put a spell on me?"

We laughed as I pulled them into a warm embrace.

"Let's clean up and then sleep. Tomorrow we can spend all day together and get dinner before going back to the village." Rhône rolled from the bed and walked to the bathroom. They threw a wet cloth at me. "Wipe up."

Once clean, we wrapped up in blankets and curled together on my bed. Within moments, I fell into the soundest and most content sleep of my life.

FIVE

"GOOD MORNING," I whispered in Rhône's ear.

"Ugnh," they mumbled and buried their head in the pillow.

"Not a morning person, huh?"

Rhône grunted.

"I'll shower and fix tea. You like tea? I think I may have coffee."

"Tea is fine. Can I shower after you?"

"Yep." I kissed the top of their head before rolling from bed and heading to the shower. My apartment wasn't exactly a studio, but it was very open with only part of the bathroom separated by a door. I hadn't ever really had overnight guests, so I was realizing there was very little privacy. At least the toilet and shower were private enough.

"Pretty sure what we did last night negates the need

to worry about privacy too much," Rhône called from their cocoon on the bed.

I glanced at my red-cheeks, in the mirror and smiled as I recalled last night. "True that," I replied.

By the time I exited the shower, Rhône had made their way to my tiny kitchenette and was fixing tea.

"Hey, you don't have to do that." I pulled their back to my front and kissed their neck.

"You can make breakfast. But if I left you to make the tea, I'd end up with pathetic Earth dweller tea." Rhône messed with whatever they had in front of them.

"What? Tea isn't pathetic."

"No, tea is great when it's done correctly. But most outsiders don't make tea the right way and don't use the proper ingredients."

"Ohhh, well, teach me, great tea master," I teased.

Rhône launched into Proper Tea 101. "Tap water is acceptable, but you should let it run for a while to aerate it. And only boil it once to keep the oxygen at the proper level. And let it steep. Goodness, it takes time for the flavor to properly form. If you're using a bag, squeeze it before removing it from the mug, but only once or the tea will get bitter. Although, I prefer loose leaf."

I gawked. "Wow, you really do know your tea prep, huh?"

Rhône shrugged. "It's not that hard. I feel that if you're going to take the time to make a cup of tea, you should make a *proper* cup of tea."

"Sorry, I don't have any loose-leaf tea. I don't know how to use that. Doesn't it get all gross in the water? Do you drink the leaves?"

Rhône laughed. "Oh, sweet Kellan. You've been deprived all this time. I'm here to save you from your tea." They finished whatever prep they'd been working on. "You fix breakfast. I'll shower. Then I'll make you a *good* cup of tea."

I busied myself with filling bowls of cereal and readying the bread for toasting.

When Rhône returned to the kitchen, I gestured toward the counter. "Sorry, I don't usually have guests for breakfast. Is cereal and toast okay?"

Rhône hugged me. "Any meal you'd like to make is perfectly fine. Plus, I see *real* butter and cinnamon sugar for the toast, so I'm thrilled."

"Is real butter one of those *proper* things?" I popped the bread into the toaster.

"Of course. That synthetic junk is terrible."

"And you like cinnamon sugar?"

"Cinnamon sugar toast is something I've loved since I was a child. My parents fixed it for me because they knew outsider children liked it. Of course, we use our own organic ingredients when possible, and the toast is made from homemade bread, but I absolutely adore cinnamon sugar toast. It makes me feel like a kid again."

"Perfect." I kissed them. "So, tell me about this tea."

Rhône set my electric kettle to boil. "Well, aside

from all I mentioned earlier, the tea is the most important. I like black tea the best, but green or herbal is perfectly fine." They pulled a small parcel from their bag. "We make our own tea."

"Of course, you do," I teased.

"Much of the actual tea comes from the outer world, but we fix it up to our liking." Rhône shook a little baggie.

"What's in it?"

Rhône poured some of the mixture into their hand and showed it to me.

I pushed the leaves around in their hand and gasped. "Are those popid petals?"

Rhône smiled and filled two small brown paper bags with the tea. "The popid is a very useful plant. We use it in a variety of ways."

"Is this going to make me high?"

They laughed and poured the hot water over the tea bags. "No, the popid petals used in this tea will not make you high."

"But the popid in general could?" I grabbed the toast when it popped and smeared butter on it.

Rhône shrugged. "Depends on how it's being used. The popid is not the same as a poppy flower. While the popid *does* have medicinal, narcotic, and recreational uses, it does *not* produce opium like the poppy. Crossing the poppy with the orchid and blending in our magic allowed us to make a plant and flower with well over a thousand uses. Yet, if it were to get in the wrong hands, dangerous drugs could be derived from it, but as it is, it's useful and safe."

"Okay. I mean, I'm not a total prude, but I mostly steer clear of drugs. I take the government-approved natural mood and health enhancers, but that's about it." I grimaced. "Okay, so that's not to say I haven't used the government-approved marijuana before. But honestly, I hate the thought of getting hold of the wacky weed or worse and getting totally messed up, so I pretty much don't participate."

I sprinkled the toast with cinnamon sugar before placing the finished pieces next to the bowls of cereal. Grabbing spoons and milk, I prepared the cramped table as best I could.

Rhône finished prepping the mugs of tea and carried them to the table, as well.

We sat, hips, thighs, and shoulders bumping, and then we grinned at our beautiful breakfast spread.

"This is really nice," Rhône whispered.

"Sorry it's not super fancy or whatever you're used to."

"Don't ever apologize. This place is you. This meal was made by your hands, from your heart. There's nowhere I'd rather be, no one I'd rather be with." Rhône kissed me. "Let's eat."

We made small-talk over our food before I cleared the table.

"So, is tea the ready?" I rubbed my hands together.

"Moment of truth. Will this forever change my tea-drinking experience?"

"If this isn't the best tea you've ever had, I'll do the dishes." Rhône sipped at their tea and sighed deeply. "Heavenly."

I took a small drink. And then another. And another. "Best. Tea. Ever."

Rhône smirked. "Guess you're doing the dishes."

We spent several minutes enjoying our tea before I cleaned up the dishes.

"You should know…as long as you don't let it get out, I'll get you any mood and health enhancers you might need from the village. We produce much more natural and effective products." Rhône winked. "And our medical marijuana is a thousand times better than anything your government has approved. Just so you know."

I laughed. "Did you just offer to be my drug dealer?"

Rhône rolled their eyes. "*Natural* drugs. For your mental, emotional, and physical health. But yes, I did. The popid will change your life."

"Hey, change of subject, but what do you want to do today?"

"Perhaps travel away from the government center? Visit one of the more outer areas?"

My eyes bugged. "How far out are you talking?"

Rhône chuckled and shook their head. "I don't mean the barren and dangerous areas, just a few miles out. Where we can find the small shops and restaurants. The ones your government doesn't *like,* but pretty much leaves alone. No one in the government wants to venture from their precious government center where they rule everything."

I nodded. "Okay, that's totally doable. I like those areas. I just don't go into the farther areas where there's so much danger."

"Yes, those who live so far out must fight for survival in ways you and I have never experienced." Rhône sighed. "Such a shame that your government made it such. My understanding is that those in the farthest areas must fight for food, shelter, clothing, every basic necessity."

"Yeah, so unfair. How does the government have the right to decide who the 'undesirables' are?" I frowned and tried to shake off the negativity that seemed to have settled around us.

"I'm sorry, I've made you sad," Rhône whispered and took my face in their hands before kissing me softly.

I breathed Rhône's soft, unique scent deep and opened my mouth to allow zir to deepen the kiss. When I was convinced we should just go back to bed for the rest of the day, Rhône pulled away. I groaned.

"Tonight," they murmured against my lips.

"Fine, shopping and lunch. But *tonight,*" I growled and hugged them tightly against me.

———

WE SPENT the day going in and out of about a thousand tiny little shops outside of the main government center. Rhône delighted in trinkets, baked goods, soaps, paintings, blown glass, leather goods, wine, chocolate, vintage clothing, and books. Their "ooohs" and "aaahs" were adorable, and I wanted to buy every single thing they picked up and went gaga over.

"It would be wasteful to spend your hard-earned money on things that I, for the most part, don't need or could make myself," Rhône argued when I got frustrated over zir not letting me purchase soap and a blown glass flower.

"This is our first real date, will you please let me buy you *something* to commemorate the occasion?" I prodded.

"Fine," Rhône huffed while we browsed a vintage store. They picked a long-sleeve, tunic-like top with a leather rope belt. "I very much enjoy this shirt and would be happy to think of you every time I wear it."

"Pick a book to go with it," I urged.

Rhône humored me and picked up a copy of *The Secret Garden*. "What?" they asked when I gave them a look.

"My Rhône, who lives in a hidden underground cave with fields of popids and other plants, chooses a book about a secret garden?" I teased.

Rhône shrugged. "It's a good story."

I smirked and paid for the items, feeling proud that I was able to give Rhône something they wanted.

As we left the shop, a thought occurred. "Do Popids have the same type of money?"

Rhône shook their head. "We *do* have a supply of Earth dweller money and ways to obtain more for times we need to participate in the outer world's commerce, but within the village, we do *not* use your money system. Popids live in peace and harmony; money is the root of many evils, and we choose to live without it."

We roamed past a bakery with cookies displayed in the front window. "What if you want a cookie? You don't have to pay for it? How does the baker in your village afford to buy more ingredients if they aren't being paid for their product?"

Rhône smiled softly. "Your money system is so engrained in your mind. Popids all have a skill, a trade, products and services they can offer. We barter. Much of our possessions are shared among the community. We share, we borrow, we trade. It works very nicely. No one is rich, no one is poor, no one has more, no one goes without."

The concept was hard to wrap my head around, but it sounded so much easier and more relaxed than the world in which I lived.

"It really is easier," Rhône teased and bumped my hip as they read my thoughts.

I put my arm around their shoulder and pulled them

close. "Speaking of cookies, I'm hungry. What should we eat?"

Rhône turned bright eyes toward me and bit their lip. "I don't want to sound greedy or piggish, but I would love a cheeseburger. We don't often have meat in the village, and I have a craving for a big juicy burger with pickles, cheese, and ketchup. Along with cinnamon sugar toast, cheeseburgers are one of my outer world weaknesses."

"That sounds amazing."

We walked a few streets over and found a small diner-like establishment which boasted of the best cheeseburgers for a hundred miles.

Rhône laughed. "Much farther out there are no restaurants, let alone good cheeseburgers. And most restaurants near the government center are required to make only the healthiest government-approved foods. So, it's quite possible it's the best cheeseburger for a hundred miles because it's the *only* cheeseburger for a hundred miles."

I laughed and took their hand while we waited for the hostess to acknowledge us. When she finally did, it was with a look of scorn at our joined hands. With a curl of her lip, the hostess snarled, "Where would you *gentlemen*"—she paused with an evil grin—"or are you a *lady?*...Whatever you are, where would you like to sit?"

Rhône stood taller and gripped my hand tighter.

I immediately bristled and fought the urge to lash

out. "We'd like a table with privacy where we don't have to worry about *rude* people."

The hostess rolled her eyes and grabbed two menus. "This way."

Once she had seated us in the farthest corner, she tossed the menus onto the table. "You're all by yourselves back here. No one to gawk at anything *freakish* or *unnatural*."

"What a complete and total bitch," I mumbled when we were alone.

Rhône reached for my hand. "I'm sorry," they began.

"Don't you *ever* apologize for who you are."

"Let me finish. I'm sorry you had to hear and see that. Sadly, that was a very mild case of my norm whenever I'm outside of the village." Rhône shrugged.

"Are you serious? People act like that all the time around you?" I asked in disgusted disbelief.

"Every day, most encounters, and practically every moment there are rude words, gawking stares, suggestive gestures, offensive questions." Rhône squeezed my hand. "It's not pleasant. I have the chance to go back to the popids and my village, which strengthens my positive powers. But you aren't used to the hatred. I'd understand if you wanted to leave or not go out in public with me. We can boost your positivity back at the village, if needed."

"Are you kidding me?" I frowned. "No way. If anything, this cements my desire to spend time with you. I don't want you going anywhere and having to deal with this type of shit alone."

Rhône caressed my hand. "Kellan, while I appreciate your intentions and protectiveness, I'm quite capable of taking care of myself. I've been dealing with humans like that hostess my entire life."

I squeezed Rhône's hand. "I one hundred percent believe you can take care of yourself. You are a strong, smart, independent person. And, I imagine, you could always magic your way out of a bad or dangerous situation." We both laughed. "But that doesn't mean it's wrong for me to want to protect you from rude assholes."

"Okay, okay. I see your point," Rhône agreed. "Just don't start acting like I'm some weakling who needs a strong outer world male to take care of me."

"Promise, that's the last thing I'd ever think or do."

The waitress finally arrived to take our order and was thankfully much friendlier than the hostess.

Rhône and I snacked on small, round pieces of fried cheese while we waited for our meals. When the plates were finally set before us, we laughed at the huge amount of food.

"Wow, this place doesn't scrimp on getting the 'authentic' feel of *American* meals of the past, huh?" I knew from my parents' stories that the former America did not have the best eating habits. Large portions of unhealthy foods had been a daily habit for many and often the cause of many health problems.

"As terrible as I'll feel later, I'm pretty sure I'll be able to demolish this burger. Maybe not all the fries, but the burger is in true danger." Rhône grabbed their knife and cut the burger in half before reaching for the ketchup and squirting a large amount all over the gigantic pile of fries.

"Whoa, whoa, what are you doing?" I laughed in fake horror.

Rhône stabbed a helping of fries with their fork, but paused with it halfway to their mouth when I spoke. "What?"

"Ketchup all over the fries? Eating fries with a fork? Travesty," I teased.

Rhône quirked a brow. "And how do you propose fries be eaten?"

I squirted a large amount of ketchup onto my plate and dipped a few fries into the condiment before popping them into my mouth. "Dipping fries and eating them with your fingers is the right way. The only *true* way."

Rhône chuckled and rolled their eyes. "To each their own I guess." And they took another large forkful of fries into their mouth before turning their attention to the burger.

Thirty minutes later, our stomachs beyond full, I paid the bill, and we wandered back out into the street.

"Oh, my goodness, I'm so full. We need to walk around for a while, or I may be sick," Rhône suggested and reached for my hand.

By the time I'd walked off my lunch, my jaw hurt from clenching, and I was ready to throat-punch the next person who said something rude to myself or Rhône. I refused to even think the offensive words, comments, and questions that had been hurled at us during our walk. I wouldn't give life to the words or the hateful bigots who had spoken them.

"Kellan, you must center yourself and calm down. Your anger is unhealthy."

"It's just wrong, and it pisses me off so much, and I *hate* that judgmental, hateful, harmful, terrible people are still in the world."

"But you cannot let their words and their hate control you and win." Rhône reached for my hand as we settled in the car. "We must fight back with positivity, with good, with love and acceptance."

"Just not feeling very loving and positive right now." I gripped the steering wheel.

"We will go to the village for a gathering, and you will feel much better."

"But I thought we had plans tonight." I tried not to sound too whiney.

Rhône chuckled. "We'll keep our plans. Just a stop by the village first."

SIX

"WOW," I whispered when we arrived at the village. "Is it possible I already feel better?"

"Yes, very much so." Rhône took my hand. "The village is surrounded by positivity. The popids, the magic, our love and acceptance, all of it should bring you happiness and peace." They pulled me along to where a large group was gathering by the popid field. "But participating in an actual gathering will make you feel even better. And more importantly, the more positive and peaceful *you* and *we* feel, the more of that we can send to Mother Earth."

"So, your gatherings are to help the village but also to help the earth?"

"Yes, our village, the popids, our people, we all benefit from the positive vibes—peace, acceptance, love, and celebrating diversity—but we also pay our respects, worship, and lift up our Mother Earth with all that we gain through a gathering." Rhône put a finger to zir lips. "It's started. We will join. Open your mind, your heart, and allow the anger, hostility, and negativity to leave your soul so that you may have room for only the good." They kissed me softly.

Over the next hour, I thought my heart would burst from the goodness surrounding me. The Popids really knew how to make a person feel welcome.

"They wouldn't be this way with just any outsider. While we are very accepting, we must also protect ourselves. The village has read you and knows you're safe. They recognize your goodness," Rhône whispered.

Singing, dancing, and stories reigned. Individuals were given special attention and an extra helping of the feel-good vibes.

"How do they know which villagers are in the most need of the boost?"

Rhône gave me a look.

"Oh, right. Empaths, magic, charms, all that stuff. My bad."

We laughed.

"If there really *is* a traitor, could the other villagers read them and uncover them?"

"Hypothetically, yes. But the traitor more than likely has cloaked their work in charms to keep their actions hidden." Rhône frowned. "We have our most trusted and skilled members working to uncover the breach."

The gathering appeared to be wrapping up. "Is that all?"

"They will end with coming together and sending all of our good to Mother Earth."

"Do you need to join them?"

"No, we can simply watch. But while everyone *is* happy and feeling good, it's a fairly serious moment, so we should be silent."

We stood silently while the rest of the villagers gathered together to send their—offering? Was that the right word? —to Mother Earth. A quiet and serene moment, but the positive feelings never left the area.

"Are you ready to go back to your place?" Rhône asked when it was over.

"We can stay here if you'd like," I offered. In reality, I wouldn't have minded staying in the village forever.

"We had plans, remember?" Rhône bumped against me. "And while sex is definitely celebrated here, I'd prefer the privacy of your apartment. Unless you're into having the whole village possibly hearing us?"

My eyes bugged. "Um, no. My apartment sounds great."

We said our goodbyes and headed out of the cave.

"So, sex isn't private in the village? People watch? Listen?"

Rhône chuckled. "Not so much, unless you're into public sex. But the village is very open. There aren't a ton of places to find *real* privacy outside of the dormitory rooms. And even then, without some charms, we'd be heard."

"I'm not against a little public sex...someday." I

pulled Rhône close to my side. "But I'd like to have you all to myself tonight."

"Then let's get to your place." Rhône's words were raspy as they spoke against my neck before kissing my ear.

———

WE TUMBLED through the door a tangle of arms, legs, lips, and tongues. When I stubbed my toe, we both laughed, and Rhône pulled away.

"Since we've been out all day, and we have all night, could I shower before we go any further?" They bit their lip as they ran a hand down my torso before cupping my balls.

"Sure, and maybe we talk a bit about what we like, what we're into, what we want from tonight?" I suddenly was beyond nervous.

Rhône leaned in and kissed me, sucking my tongue into their mouth. "Of course, and if we do no more than we did before, that's fine." Licking my bottom lip, Rhône continued, "But I'd very much like to take things a little further. Maybe a lot further."

I wrapped them in my arms, relishing the feeling of perfection which came with holding Rhône. "Let me jump in and rinse off first, then you can take as long as you'd like." I winced. "But the hot water won't hold out for long."

Twenty minutes later, I lounged on the bed, doing

my best to control my thoughts and the raging hard-on in my boxers. Rhône had hinted at topping me. Would they want to do that tonight? I'd experienced a little anal play with a few people, but I'd never had full-on anal sex. Rhône was very well endowed, would it hurt? I was nervous, but so very curious. Just the thought of them sliding into my ass had me squeezing my length and trying to stop myself from coming.

"Kellan, we don't have to do anything you're not comfortable with," Rhône spoke from the edge of the room. Completely naked, damp hair pulled up on top of their head, fist stroking their cock.

"Come here," I demanded and moved to my knees on the bed. I opened my arms, and Rhône walked into my embrace. "I want you. Any way. Every way. For always."

"Let's set our boundaries." Rhône pushed us both to the bed.

We lay on our sides, facing each other.

Rhône touched my face. "Tonight, I'd prefer to bottom for you. And I want anal only. I don't want to have to protect against pregnancy. I want all of my focus on you tonight. When was your last STD test?"

I gulped, so fucking turned on over what Rhône wanted from me. "Um, I've had two since Dayne and I broke up, and I've not been with anyone since then."

"I'm also free of any infections," Rhône stated, their hand caressing my hip. "If we aren't worried about pregnancy, and you're okay with it, you can take me bare."

I could only nod.

"What do you want?"

When I stammered, Rhône saved me from myself.

"Are you okay with no condoms?"

I nodded.

"Are you okay with anal sex?"

I nodded again.

"Kellan, I need to hear the words. And I need you to snap out of whatever lust-induced trance you're in."

I shook my head to clear it. "Sorry, I'm a little overwhelmed. You're so damn amazing, so beautiful, and I want to be with you so badly. I am on board with any type of sex you want. And I *do* want to bottom for you, soon."

Rhône smiled and reached for my throbbing cock and then kissed me.

There was nothing about their body I didn't love. Soft, angular, muscular, fragile, I loved every area. I poured myself into the kiss and gathered Rhône's energy as my hands roamed their body.

Rhône moved quickly and positioned their face right at my cock. As they took me deep into their warm, wet mouth, I gripped their pulsing cock and licked. Every time I thrust my dick between Rhône's lips, they rocked into my mouth. I moaned as we reached a perfect rhythm.

"Kel, I want you inside me, I want to come with

your cock deep in my ass," Rhône begged and rolled to their back. "Please."

I moved so I was between Rhône's legs. Trailing two fingers into the wetness from their center, pressing deep and feeling their body clench around me, I spread the wetness to their ass and teased their hole with my slick finger.

"I want your cock, Kel, please," Rhône writhed under me, fisting their cock, and rocking their ass against my hand.

I grabbed a pillow, propped Rhône's ass up, and spread their legs. Their body, throbbing cock, wet center, tight pink hole, all on display, almost brought me to release. I gripped my cock and squeezed. Lubing myself with Rhône's fluid, I pressed the tip of my dick into their body. Slowly, painfully slowly, I inched into Rhône and watched in amazement as their body opened for me and took me in.

Rhône had one hand on their cock, one arm over their head gripping a pillow, and eyes wide open as they watched me take their body.

Perfection.

No union had ever been so exquisite.

Our differences were nothing. I knew only that my heart, my soul, my body had found its forever.

"Kellan, move please. Fuck me. I need it," Rhône pleaded.

I withdrew and thrust forcefully back into their heat and delighted in Rhône's whimpers and moans. Setting a pace, I continued the forceful thrusting until Rhône exploded all over their chest. Their ass constricting around my length was all it took before I was spilling into their body with a final thrust and moan.

Not wanting to crush them, I reached for some tissue and cleaned myself and Rhône before gathering them in my arms and holding them close. "Rhône, baby, was that okay? Are you okay?"

Rhône nodded into my chest. "Kellan, I'm a magical being. I can make *a lot* of things *very* good. But nothing in my life has ever rocked my soul and my inner being, like our joining."

I breathed a sigh of relief. "Whew, good. I felt the same. That was so far beyond amazing."

I fell into an exhausted but satisfied sleep.

———

WHEN THE MORNING sun began to filter through the window, I woke enough to recognize Rhône was still in my arms, but they had turned during the night, and now their back was to me.

Which left my very awake cock pressed against their naked ass.

"Do it, Kel, slide deep in my ass and fuck me," Rhône whispered.

I almost shot my load right then. Rhône adopting the rough, crass words I knew weren't natural for them did crazy things to me.

Lifting Rhône's left leg, I fingered their core and stroked their cock before nudging my throbbing head against their tight hole. Pressing, retreating, and teasing, I finally slipped inside. How Rhône's body was hotter, tighter, more intense than the night before, I'd never know. Our morning joining was slower, softer, but no less intimate and incredible.

Later, we roused from bed and took a long, leisurely shower until the hot water ran out. I learned that I had enough hot water for two blow jobs. *Who knew?*

Once we were dried off and mostly dressed, Rhône spoke softly as we assembled something like a breakfast. "I do want us to try other types of sex, but having you take me like that was so perfect. I'd be happy with that forever."

"And as much as I really want to experience you taking *me* like that, I'd be perfectly satisfied with last night for the rest of my life." I paused and frowned. "Actually, as amazing as penetrating you was, I'd be completely fine with kissing and blow jobs for the rest of my life. It's so strange how just being *with* you is as satisfying as anything sexual."

"Agreed." Rhône kissed me. "But I'd still like to fuck your ass," they whispered, using the crass slang, and my knees almost buckled.

"Anytime," I assured and returned the kiss.

We enjoyed breakfast of cinnamon sugar toast and *proper* tea.

"I think we should go back to the village and visit," I suggested.

Rhône smiled and rolled their eyes. "Good thing I know you like me, or I'd think you were just with me for the village."

"Well, that and the popids," I teased.

Rhône bumped me lightly with their fist and stuck out their tongue.

I lunged and captured their mouth, sucking their tongue between my lips.

Rhône tickled my sides.

I immediately gave up. "Stop, stop, I'm sorry." I laughed and tried to wiggle away from them.

"Oh, is my Kellan ticklish?" Rhône teased.

"Very," I agreed.

"Interesting. Good to know." Rhône wrapped their arms around my neck. "I promise to use the knowledge only for good." They kissed me. "Mostly."

SEVEN

"KELLAN, we're so glad to have you back." Rube wrapped an arm around me and squeezed before releasing me.

Nayel hugged Rhône before pulling me into the embrace.

"Come, let's have tea. We'd like to talk to you," Nayel suggested and headed toward the kitchen area.

"Oh my God, is this a, 'What are your intentions with our child' type talk?" I whispered to Rhône.

Rhône threw back their head and laughed. "No, they trust my choices. And they like you. Relax."

The tea calmed me, obviously the popids, and the conversation was enjoyable.

"Before you and Rhône go off to explore or do whatever it is you young ones like to do"— Nayel teased with a wink—"Rube and I would like to ask you some questions if you're agreeable."

I nodded. "Sure."

"You seem very open to the differences between humans and Popids. How do you explain that? You've grown up in times where differences are not well accepted and hatred is supported by the most powerful in the land. Why do you feel like you're able to be so open and accepting?"

I smiled. "My parents have always said I have the most accepting, caring, kindest heart they've ever seen. So, I think a lot of it is just my nature. But my parents also nurtured those tendencies in me. They had me right at the time where our country went from making great strides in inclusion and acceptance of *all* people, so Mom and Dad took my natural disposition and encouraged it. I was taught acceptance. I was taught to see and celebrate differences."

Nayel and Rube smiled. "You were very lucky to have such intelligent and nurturing parents." Nayel patted my knee.

"You've stated many times that you don't have any extra-sapien blood. Can you tell us how you're so certain of this?" Rube asked.

I gave the question a bit of thought. "Well, my parents aren't from paranormal, supernatural, or fantasy heritage. Neither has ever mentioned a family member with any type of extra-sapien blood. And my parents would have told me. They know how badly I want to be part of the DPSFS. Every time I apply for the department, I have to fill out the same application. I never get past the initial application process. I know others who have been denied *after* the blood test and interview portion, but I'm always denied as soon as they see my application. My entrance essay is strong, my background is clean, and my work ethic is good. I'm an ally of the extra-sapien community, so the only thing I can think is that my parentage keeps me from moving on. I mean, it makes sense." I shrugged and scrunched up my face. "No need to waste resources to do a blood test and interview when my parents aren't extra-sapien."

Nayel reached for my hand. "We would like to invite you to stay in the village for a while. With your permission, we'd like to study you. Rube and I, along with the rest of the elders, feel something different from you. We can't pinpoint it, but if we have your blessing, we'd like to dig deeper into your history, your heritage, your blood…" Nayel trailed off and looked at me with wide, hopeful eyes.

I stared at Nayel and then at Rube for several awkward moments before I could speak. "Um, I'd love to stay for a while. I'd need to ask off from work. I feel like it would be a waste of your time and energy, but of course you can study me. Maybe you'll find something interesting." I smiled and glanced toward Rhône. "Are you okay with me staying for a while?"

Rhône nodded. "Very much so."

"Well, then, I guess it's settled. Let me go home, grab some clothes and a bag, and check in with work.

I've never really taken any time off, so it shouldn't be a problem." I stood. "Rhône, do you want to go with me?"

"I'll stay here and work on some of my spells. Call me when you're close. Or you could always try thinking about me and see if I can pick up on your thoughts." They smiled and nodded at the exit. "I'll come guide you through the waterfall when you're back."

An hour later, I had notified work that I'd be out for a week. It was nice having the time accrued. I gathered clothes and toiletries and threw them into a bag. On my way back to the waterfall, I prayed I couldn't see it because I wanted the entrance safe from others. I glanced at my phone when I got a notification from the government-approved news app.

Several murders had occurred in the farthest areas of the land, the very outer rings of populated land. Very few details were available because most news crews wouldn't travel to the desolate, dangerous areas. But information was sometimes shared from the locals of the outer-most areas. Up to twenty people had been killed. No one had claimed responsibility, and no clear motive had been established. But, because the killer or killers had not been caught, the government was calling for extra safety precautions and a curfew. A list of names of the deceased was included, and anyone within the government center who had lost an immediate family member was allowed bereavement days, but were warned not to travel to the outer-most areas without protection.

A heavy sadness cloaked me. Why were we still dealing with such violence and hatred? These types of stories were pretty much a given; violence happened daily, especially in the outer rings. So, why did this information hit me so much harder? *Rhône.* Because of Rhône and the Popids. The hatred would affect them and the village.

Loud, roaring water broke into my thoughts. *Shit.* I could see the waterfall clearly. I glanced around in a panic, but none of the people in the area seemed aware. I rushed toward the waterfall and slipped behind it. *Rhône, I'm here. There's a problem. Something bad has happened and I can see the waterfall again. I'm behind it, in the cave. I'll wait here for you.*

I threw my thoughts into the purple haze and hoped Rhône could hear me.

My heart seized in my chest as if Rhône were hugging me close. Was it possible I was feeling their thoughts?

Wait for me, Kellan. I'm on my way.

Whoa, I could hear Rhône.

Within moments, Rhône came rushing up the cave's steps. "Kellan!"

"I heard your thoughts!"

"Good. I'll keep purposely throwing them to you so you can practice the skill."

I followed them down the steps where the elders

waited. They'd all seen the news. It was clear the negativity had rocked the Popids and their village. I could see the waterfall which meant it was possible for others, at least extra-sapiens, to see it. So far, it appeared I was the only nonextra-sapien to see the falls.

Building up the charms to hide the waterfall and cave was the first order of business. Between the negativity of the outer world and the possible traitor in the village, it seemed keeping the waterfall hidden and the magic working was a constant job.

Next was a gathering to worship Mother Earth and send offerings of positivity through singing, praying, chanting, and dancing.

The Popids were shaken and the village felt *off*. I was glad to be with Rhône. The safety of the village, even a shaken village, was more comforting than my tiny empty apartment.

"You should call your parents and let them know you're okay and that you'll be gone for a while," Rhône suggested. "I'm going to help with the charms. I have some new spells to try for hiding the waterfall. I'll be busy for a bit. The village is open to you. Feel free to explore, rest, or visit."

They were right. I needed to call my parents. My phone got zero reception down in the cave, so I climbed the steps to stand as close to the waterfall's edge as possible.

As I made the call, I absently willed the noise of the waterfall to quiet. *As if.*

"Kellan, are you okay? I saw the news story. Did you recognize any of the names? Dad knew one of them. They'd gone to school together." Mom's worried words rushed out as soon as she picked up.

"Mom, I'm good. I didn't know any of the names, but it doesn't make it any less horrible."

"You're right, of course." She sighed.

"Listen, I'm calling to let you know I'm okay and to tell you I took a week off work. I'm spending some time with a friend."

"A friend?"

"Okay, maybe more than a friend," I hedged.

"Boy? Girl?"

Mom and Dad were open to my pansexuality, but they still didn't completely get that my sexuality meant I was attracted to more than just male and female.

"Their name is Rhône and they are genderqueer." I smiled, and knew my mom would make a fuss over that smile. "They are the most amazing, beautiful person I've ever met, Mom."

"That's wonderful, Kellan. I'm so happy for you. Would Dad and I be able to meet him...I mean, *them*?"

My heart smiled at Mom's use of a gender-neutral pronoun.

"Definitely. But not right now. I'd like some more time with them before introducing them to friends and family."

"Of course. So, you're staying with them? Are they from around here?"

"Yes, they live nearby," I stated. It wasn't technically a lie. I just left out the part about the waterfall, the cave, and the magic.

"Well, have a nice time. Be safe, extra vigilant. Don't go to the outer areas. And tell Rhône they sound lovely and we'd love to meet them."

"Thanks, Mom. I need to go. Love you. Give Dad my best."

"Love you, too."

When I hung up, I realized I hadn't had any trouble hearing my mom over the sound of the waterfall, and she hadn't once mentioned the noise. Yet, the water crashed and echoed around the cave as clearly as ever.

Weird.

———

THE POPIDS SPENT the next several hours strengthening the charms and reworking vital spells. By the time everyone came together for the gathering, exhaustion and tension were evident on many faces.

An elderly villager came around with a tray of small cups.

"Take one," Rhône whispered.

"What is it?" I didn't think the Popids would offer anything dangerous, but I never ate or drank anything without knowing what I was putting in my body.

"Popid juice concentrate. It will ease fear, anxiety, and bring energy."

"It's not illegal?"

"Kellan, your government doesn't control our popid fields or the products we make from them."

"If they knew about it, would they make it illegal?"

"I'd like to think they'd recognize the health benefits and treat it as they do medical marijuana." Rhône shrugged and swigged the liquid. "Trust me."

I did. With my life. Which was odd because I'd *never* trusted anyone that way except maybe my parents. I took the small cup and swallowed the juice. It was as if I'd tasted the nectar of the gods. The elixir of life.

Rhône snorted. "Settle down, it's not *that* amazing."

Within several moments, the village had perked up thanks to the popid juice. The gathering began solemnly, acknowledging the victims of the recent violence, sending comfort to their families and friends, and asking for knowledge and sight to find those responsible. Slowly, the gathering turned more energetic; dancing, singing, stories, and affirmations filled the cave.

My entire being moved from a somewhat sad, somewhat neutral emotional state to feeling warm, peaceful, positive, and loved. I was allowed to participate in the ending ritual, which sent the offering to Mother Earth. I'd never felt so connected, so a part of something, so just plain old *good*.

Later, Rhône and I lay cuddled on the bed in their private quarters. The room was very minimalist; only the needed basics and very few decorations.

"So, you've charmed the room? We have some privacy?" I glanced toward the door.

"Yes," Rhône answered and kissed my nose. "Relax. No one can accidentally walk in, and no one can hear us."

"Why didn't you do this the other night?"

Rhône shrugged and smiled. "I wanted to see your place, spend time in your bed."

I laughed and swatted their ass. "You sure your parents are okay with me being in your bed?"

Rhône rolled zir eyes. "I'm an adult, and I'm one of the most respected members of this village. My parents, even if they wanted to, don't control who is in my bed." They kissed me. "Do you have more questions?"

I lowered my eyes.

Rhône raised a brow.

"You said you sometimes enjoy vaginal penetration," I murmured, "but protecting yourself against pregnancy was an issue. Tell me more about all of that."

Rhône was quiet for a moment. "I often feel mostly masculine. I often choose to have anal sex with a male because it's what I desire. But sometimes, I feel very feminine, very maternal, and I dream about carrying a child." Rhône sighed. "It's why I've not done any permanent protection."

"You can do that?"

"Very similar to females in your world doing permanent birth control," Rhône replied. "But I've not yet ruled out wanting to carry a child. And sometimes having sex the way a female would is what I want and what feels good. It's what makes my body so ideal." Rhône threw a leg over my hip and rocked their stiff cock into mine. "But right now, I very much want our mouths sucking each other's cocks until we explode. I love to taste you on my tongue."

I flipped my position so our faces were level with each other's groins.

"Did you know this used to be referred to as *sixty-nine*?" Rhône asked.

"Yeah." I nuzzled my nose against their bulge and breathed deeply. "I guess I can see the similarity to the number. Now, no more talking." I slid Rhône's pants down to reveal their heavy cock. Licking the glistening slit, I swirled my tongue around the head just as Rhône released my erection from my pants.

With no warning, Rhône gripped my ass and engulfed my cock, taking me to the back of their throat. The gagging sound Rhône made shouldn't have turned me on as much as it did. I pulled from their dick to watch as my throbbing, dark flesh impaled and stretched their beautiful pink lips.

"Suck me," Rhône groaned and gripped their cock before shoving it into my mouth.

We set a hot, wet, frantic rhythm of lips, tongues, and thrusting cocks before slicking our fingers and teasing each other's holes.

"Can I lick you?" Rhône asked.

"Like rimming?"

Rhône nodded, and I moaned.

"Only if I can do the same?"

"Yes, please," Rhône whispered.

We shifted our positions so we could tongue the other's tight hole.

I probed and thrust deep, but lost focus and cried out when Rhône's tongue breached my body. My balls drew up tight, and I knew I wasn't going to last much longer.

"I'm going to come if you do that too many more times," I warned.

Rhône moved swiftly to push me to my back and straddled me. "Take my ass, please. I want your release inside of me." Zie reached behind and guided my cock to their hole.

"Oh, fuck," I gasped as my head encountered that first ring of resistance.

Rhône rocked slightly and their body gave in to allow my invasion.

"So, fucking tight. So hot," I growled and thrust upwards.

"Touch me," Rhône demanded as they rode my cock.

I licked my palm, gripped the hot flesh of their dick, and pumped as Rhône reached behind to tease my balls.

I sat up and moved Rhône's legs to wrap around my waist while my legs hung over the edge of their bed. "Fuck yourself on me, baby," I commanded.

I held them close, our bodies trapping their cock between us, and thrust hard into their ass.

Our orgasms ripped from us, fast, hot, blinding until we were left quivering in each other's arms.

"Oh my God," I mumbled against Rhône's chest. "I will *never* get tired of that."

"Same," Rhône agreed and sighed.

We cleaned up and settled into bed again.

I pulled Rhône close. "I know the village is perfect, and you don't *need* the outer world, but what from the outer world intrigues you the most?"

When Rhône paused, I raised my brow in expectation.

"You really want to know? And promise not to laugh?"

"Of course, I want to know everything about you."

"I have a top three," Rhône admitted. "First, is love letters. With technology, maybe they don't get used that much anymore, but love letters seem so intimate and romantic."

I smiled and kissed them. "Maybe I'll write you a long sappy love letter someday. What's number two?"

Rhône blushed. "Slow dancing. We dance in the village all the time, but it's happy and energetic. Soft, slow music, holding each other, that just seems lovely."

"Mmmm," I murmured against their head. "Definitely something we can remedy. Number three?"

Rhône bit zir lip. "A strip tease. Having someone do one for me, just for me, seems intimate and erotic."

"Noted." I rolled from the bed. "Come on. We're taking care of one of those right now."

"Are you stripping for me?" Rhône's eyes grew wide.

"Maybe someday, but I'll need some practice. And maybe some popid enhancer." I grabbed their phone, turned on some soft music, and held out my hand. "Would you like to dance?"

Rhône's eyes filled with tears as they walked into my arms.

I held them in my embrace and swayed them gently side to side.

Rhône sobbed against my chest.

"Hey, baby, what's wrong?" I tipped their chin to look at me.

"Please don't freak out," Rhône pleaded.

"Never, what's wrong? I didn't mean to make you cry."

"I'm falling in love with you." Rhône's cheeks glistened with tears.

My heart stopped. I ran their words through my head. "Is that all?" Placing a kiss on top of their head, I chuckled. "Way ahead of you, baby."

Rhône arched a brow.

"I'm not just falling in love with you, I'm *already* in love with you." The words tumbled from my mouth and I meant every single one. "I love you, Rhône."

"You do? Despite my body being so different from what you're used to? Despite the magic? Despite the hiding?"

"*Because* of your body. It's perfect and amazing, and we fit together so perfectly, both physically and emotionally. *Because* of your magic. I've always been drawn to anything extra-sapien. I want to learn from you even if I'm not one of you. *Because* of the hiding. The outer world is sad and dangerous. I love the refuge I've found in your world." I sealed my words with a soft kiss, tracing Rhône's lips with my tongue. "I love you. Everything about you."

Rhône took a deep, shuddering breath. "I love you, too, Kellan. So very much. I don't like the reasons for *why* you were able to follow me here that day, but I'm so very grateful we met."

"Even without the broken spells, I'd like to think we would have someday met."

Rhône sighed and rested their cheek against my chest.

We danced without words, in a loving and connected silence, for several more moments.

"We should sleep. There's work to do tomorrow." Rhône pulled me to the bed.

Goodnight, Kellan.

I sat bolt upright. "Did you just say something?"

Rhône giggled. "No, why." *I love you, Kellan. Now go to sleep.*

"Oh my God! I can hear you! I heard you earlier, but I thought that was because of the danger." I rolled over on top of them. "Are you saying things in your head or purposely pushing your thoughts to me?"

Rhône laughed again. "Yes. I've been doing it since we met, pushing the thoughts your way, but today and tonight is the first time you've either been *able* to hear me, or your mind has been open to hearing me."

"Fuck, this is absolutely amazing! I'll have to keep working on hearing you. Maybe one day I'll be able to hear you without your purposely sending the thoughts my way."

"Yes, keep practicing, and maybe one day you will." Rhône kissed me.

Wrapped in each other's arms, we fell asleep happy and in love.

EIGHT

THE NEXT DAY, I snuck to a private corner of the cave and penned a love letter to Rhône. I didn't know when I would give it to them, but I knew I wanted to write it and share my love for them.

Dear Rhône,

I'm so very lucky to have you in my life. My life was fine before you, steady and somewhat comfortable. But the day I met you changed everything for me. Being with you makes me realize how simple and bland my life was before. I smile brighter, feel better, and see things with such a better view, all because of you. (Don't try to convince me it's the popids. YOU, Rhône, are what has changed me, made me so much better, made me so much happier, gave me hope for an actual meaningful future.)

When I came out as pansexual, I knew it meant that I found myself attracted to more than just male and female genders. I knew I was attracted to any individual with a good heart, a kind spirit, a welcoming and open personality. But I sometimes wondered if I'd ever find someone who fit that description. And then I met you.

Yes, your magic and powers make you intriguing and amazing and so very wonderful. But even without all of that, I'd be in love with your heart, your soul, your spirit. No one in my life has ever been as good and kind and phenomenal as you. My heart, my soul, and my spirit found their home, their anchor, their perfect match. Until you, I didn't believe in love at first sight. Until you, I didn't think souls could fuse in such an utterly exquisite way.

You are my other half, my missing piece, my love at first sight, my soul mate. I would give up anything for you. I would fight for you. I would die for you. You are my heart, my future, my everything. I love you, and if you'll have me, I'll spend the rest of my life showing you how much I love you.

Love,

Kellan

A FEW DAYS LATER, we were working with some of the village children. "I'm really glad you had me come with you today. These kids are amazing." I stood close to Rhône's side and watched as several young Popids worked on various projects. Many were practicing spells and charms, some were creating recipes with the popid flower, some were carving or building with wood, and still others were reading and writing while another group worked on their physical trainings.

"I'm glad you wanted to come. The children are fun,

and they are definitely happy to have you here," Rhône teased. "Many are quite aflutter with you around."

I blushed. "Well, I hope they realize I'm much too old for them."

Rhône elbowed me. "I'd like to think you're also unavailable."

"Oh, yeah, that too," I quipped.

Rhône frowned to hide a smile. *You're mine, don't forget it.*

"I'm joking. I'm joking." I pulled them close to my side.

Rhône stood on tiptoes and kissed my cheek. "We'll have lunch soon. Maybe work in the popids later?"

"Good, I'm starving. And I'd love to work in the popids."

When Rhône went to check on a group, I found a child working on their own.

"Hey, would you do me a favor?" I whispered and nearly laughed at the wide eyes turned my way.

The child nodded. "Yes, of course. Anything you need, Kellan. I can do it. Just ask. Well, I mean, *anything* as long as it doesn't break the village rules. And as long as it's not something about my skills. But almost anything. Yes." They rambled without even a breath.

I chuckled. "When Rhône comes back, can you give this to them? But don't tell them it's from me." I handed the kid a folded-up piece of paper.

"What if they ask where it came from?"

I smiled. "Tell them Cupid delivered it."

The young Popid scrunched up their nose, but took the paper. "Who's Cupid?"

"What's your name?"

"Dmi," the young Popid answered with a proud smile.

"How much do you know of ancient mythology?"

Dmi shrugged. "A little maybe."

"Cupid was the god of love in ancient mythology," I explained.

"The god of *love?*" Dmi's cheeks blushed pink.

I winked. "Can you make sure that paper gets to Rhône?"

Dmi nodded. "Yes, I will make sure."

A few moments later, Rhône returned, and I busied myself with a group using popids in recipes. I forced myself not to look toward Rhône.

When we broke for lunch, Rhône grabbed my hand and pulled me into a small corner. Tears filled their eyes.

"Hey, hey, it's okay," I cooed. "It wasn't supposed to make you cry."

"They are happy tears." Rhône sniffed. "You wrote me a love letter?"

I tipped their chin and kissed them softly. "I'm not super great with words, but I love you and you wanted love letters, so I wrote you one."

"It was absolutely beautiful, and I'll forever cherish

every single word." Rhône wrapped their arms around my neck and hugged me tightly.

"And you're beautiful and I cherish you." I kissed them soft and deep. "Let's eat lunch."

I enjoyed every meal in the village. Everything was homegrown, fresh picked, and homemade. I'd never tasted food so flavorful and fresh. My mom was a great cook, but she could only do so much with the outer world's canned and processed foods.

I'd learned that village's mealtimes varied from day to day. Some days huge groups would gather; some days just a few sat together. Some days feasts were prepared, and some days only small meals. I had yet to determine a pattern. I was never hungry, but I never really knew what to expect.

On this day, homemade noodles, mashed potatoes, and hot, buttered rolls were placed before us.

"Oh my God, I've died and gone to Heaven," I moaned.

"No, just the Popid village," Rhône teased.

"I may need a long, cuddly nap after this," I warned.

"That won't be possible. The popid fields await."

Remembering I would help in the fields brought a smile to my face as I dug into the heavenly meal.

———

"THERE'S SO much to learn and know," I exclaimed as Rhône provided a detailed tour of the grounds as well as lessons on the popid flower. The vast popid fields stretched for as far as my eye could see. The bright purple flowers swayed in a soft breeze. And to think, only a few outer world dwellers even had an inkling of the hidden world under their feet.

"Yes, it takes many years for one to become a true expert of the popid."

Their words gave me pause. "Do Popids die?"

"The flower or the person?"

"Either, both."

"The popid flower has a very long life and normally doesn't wither until all of its many uses have been cultivated," Rhône explained. "A Popid person has a much longer lifespan than that of a human, but yes, Popids do eventually pass on."

"Pass on? So not *die* as humans?"

"Popids are believed to move from our hidden village here on your earth to a larger, more open habitat in the great beyond."

"So how long is *longer than humans?*"

"Much longer. In my time, I've only experienced the passing of one elder."

"Wow," I breathed. "Can Popids been killed?" I winced as the words left my mouth.

"The flower or the person?" Rhône quipped.

"Both."

"Popid flowers are very hearty, very difficult to kill. It's possible, but the vast majority can pull through almost anything."

"And the people?" My heart clenched at the thought that an outsider could kill Rhône or any of the villagers.

"While Popids *can* be killed, we are very much like the flower. Strong, resilient, and hearty. Our magic not only protects us, but can also be used to revive us. But staying hidden is one of our best lines of protection. We *can* be harmed and injured, in which case our healing time depends upon the injuries."

We wandered into the laboratory area where I was able to observe the gorgeous purple popid being prepared for nearly a thousand different uses. There was no way to see all the processes; it would take months to do that. But I saw popids being used for dye, flour, ink, tea, juice, seasoning, and over twenty different medicines just in the brief time we were there.

"Come, we should help the children wrap up their studies for the day." Rhône gestured for me to follow. "You're welcome to come back and observe. Some of the villagers would likely even invite you to observe or help. I think Ximon would be a good one work with." Rhône pointed toward a Popid in the far corner of the lab. "They are one of the most powerful and knowledgeable individuals in the village. They will be nominated for the elder board very soon."

Ximon looked our way. I wondered if they had heard our conversation or read our thoughts.

"We'll ask Ximon about you assisting them sometime soon," Rhône continued as they led me from the lab.

"Really? Yes, I definitely want to do that." I gave a wave to Ximon and followed Rhône.

We spent the next hour helping students finish their lessons and projects for the day. Okay, *Rhône* assisted students. I pretty much just stood around and tried not to be in the way.

"Do you guys know how to play Duck, Duck, Goose?" I asked when cleanup was done.

When the kids shook their heads, I glanced at Rhône.

With their approval, I continued. "It's an old game my parents told me about." I explained the concept of the game and helped get the kids situated. By that time, we had a crowd of villagers gathering to watch.

I realized quickly that extra-sapien beings with a variety of magical and otherwise fantastical abilities could turn a simple game of Duck, Duck, Goose into something quite enjoyable and entertaining. The few times I'd played the old game as a child definitely were nowhere as exciting as the Popids made it.

Now at the end of my week in the village, I'd come to some conclusions, which I considered as I watched the children play.

Kids, at least Popid children, were a lot of fun.

I had so much I wanted to learn.

Never had I wished so hard to have extra-sapien blood.

I wanted to spend the rest of my life with the Popids.

I was madly in love with Rhône.

A striptease was going to happen.

At my place.

I was nervous as hell.

I'd get over it for Rhône.

Deep breath, Kellan.

And...I was ready—for real, so damn ready—to bottom for Rhône.

————

"KELLAN, YOU SEEM REALLY NERVOUS," Rhône murmured into my ear and trailed kisses down my jaw. "I'll make some tea while you shower and relax a little." Zie teased at my neck with their hot tongue. "And I know what you're nervous about, but nothing has to happen that you don't want to happen."

I pulled their body tight against mine and captured zir mouth in a deep kiss, trying to pour my want into the connection between us. "I want you, so damn bad. I *am* nervous just because I've never bottomed, and I'm afraid I'll mess up somehow."

"Never." Rhône nipped at my lip. "Nothing between us, emotionally or physically, could ever be messed up. We fit together, we get each other. And I'm so ready to slide deep into your body; I want to own you the way you own me."

I wanted to get naked and offer my ass to Rhône right then.

Rhône laughed. "Tea and shower first," they teased and turned me toward the bathroom.

Would I *ever* get used to them being able to hear my thoughts?

"Probably not," Rhône called after me.

Damn.

But you can keep working on hearing mine.

I smiled. I was getting better. Or maybe Rhône was just getting better at making sure I could hear them. Either way, it was cool.

Fifteen minutes later, I walked from the bathroom wearing a tank and basketball shorts. I had a plan, but I needed that tea.

"Please tell me you put some extra calming popid power in that tea," I said as I came up behind Rhône and took them in my arms. "How do you always smell so good? Flowers, soap, sunshine, and just *you*." I took a deep breath, the scent going straight to my dick. Rhône rocked back on my erection. My hands moved from their hips to the solid length in zir soft, flowy pants. "Popid clothing doesn't hide a huge hard-on very well," I teased.

"Only slightly less well than basketball shorts." Rhône thrust their ass hard against my cock. "Plus, I have no reason to hide my desire. I want to share it with you."

I palmed their erection and nipped at zir neck. "I've never been so excited about sharing time."

"Tea first. I made sure it was strong enough to calm

your nerves." Rhône handed me a steaming mug. "And I made it sweet, just as you like it."

We stood in my small kitchen, sipping tea, with our eyes locked on each other. It shouldn't have been, but it was the most erotic foreplay I'd ever engaged in.

Rhône smirked and winked. *Soon.*

Draining my tea, I was ready to put my plan into action. I took Rhône's cup and put both mugs in the sink. Grabbing a kitchen chair, I placed it in the center of the tiny apartment. Taking Rhône's hand, I led them to the chair and kissed them deeply before pushing them gently into the chair.

My hands trembled as I thumbed through my phone for a song. I'd never done a strip tease. But if Rhône wanted one, that's what zie was going to get. The song's rhythm mixed with the relaxing vibes from the tea, which soothed some of my nerves. I turned around, and the rest of my anxiety flew out the window when I saw Rhône. Biting their lip, hands clasped at their chin, and fire in zir eyes. They were turned on and excited, and that was all that mattered to me.

I walked toward them slowly, my eyes never leaving theirs. Reaching their chair, I moved to the beat for a moment before stripping my shirt over my head. Rhône's hands trailed up my torso. I backed up, wagging a finger at them, and caressing my body. Thumbs hooked in the waistband of my shorts, I shot them a questioning look. Zie nodded, begging me with their eyes to remove the shorts. Slowly, inch by inch, beat by beat, I lowered the black material until I was standing in only a pair of boxer briefs.

Note to self: Get sexier underwear for next time.

Rhône chuckled, but fire remained in their eyes. Zir pants were tented with their erection. *Your choice of underwear is not a problem for my desire.*

I was about to bust a nut and knew I needed to finish the performance soon. The underwear came off a bit more quickly than I'd planned, and I danced slowly toward Rhône until I was within their reach. When I straddled them and rubbed my ass on their cock, my own hard length throbbing between us, Rhône moaned and snaked their arms around me to grip my ass.

"You are the most amazing, beautiful person I've ever known. I want to be inside you, *now.* Are you still okay with that?"

I rolled my ass. "Yes, so okay with that."

Rhône pressed a hand against my chest, and we both stood. They pushed me backward until my knees hit the mattress.

"You have too many clothes on." I reached for the hem of Rhône's shirt and lifted it over their head.

Zie stripped their pants off quickly, taking the light undergarment with the outer material. They pressed into me until we both fell to the bed, a pile of writhing arms and legs, caressing hands, kissing lips, teasing tongues.

"How would you like to be? On your knees? Your

back? On top of me?" Rhône stroked my cock, smearing the wetness at the tip.

"On my back. I want to see your face."

"You'd see my face if you were on top. That might make it a little less painful." Rhône's face was tight with concern.

"No, I want to lie back and open my body for you. I know you'll make it as gentle as possible."

After nodding, Rhône kissed me, thrusting their tongue deep, devouring my mouth. They reached for a bottle of lube in the nightstand. Spreading the liquid on their fingers, Rhône came back to kissing me as zie teased my hole. Slowly, pressing gently, their finger breached the tight ring of muscle. I winced at the sting, but the pain was fleeting. Rhône took their time adding another finger. The pain was more of a burn, but their tongue soothed with a kiss. The third finger took my breath, and my cock deflated slightly. Rhône knelt between my legs and continued to tease my hole with slick fingers while stroking my cock back to life.

"Please, Rhône. I want you in me," I begged, writhing against their fingers.

Rhône poured lube onto their cock, slicking it and spreading the extra into my ass. Lining up with my hole, the head of Rhône's dick pressed gently at my opening. "Kellan, I love you. Thank you for giving me this."

I tensed as Rhône entered me, slowly, a tiny bit at a

time. "Only you, Rhône. No one else gets this. I belong to you. Only you."

Zie slid the rest of the way in, my body stretching, stinging, burning as I opened for them. The heat and stretch were like nothing I'd ever felt before. It hurt, but it hurt so good. When Rhône lifted one of my legs to their shoulder, I whimpered as their cock slid even deeper. They thrust soft and slow, allowing my body to adjust to their presence.

"Do it harder," I begged.

Rhône kept the rhythm slow, but increased the force behind each thrust. "Do you want to come like this? Or after I spill inside you?"

Their words stoked the fire in me. "Make me come now. I want to come with you inside."

Rhône gripped my cock and pumped.

Between the hot cock thrusting slowly in and out of my ass and the fist stroking my own cock, I quickly lost all coherent thought. With balls drawn tight, my release exploded between us, painting my belly, my ass clenching on Rhône's dick.

Rhône cried out as I came, and began thrusting harder and faster.

"I want to feel you come inside me, fill me," I begged, my body still shuddering.

Rhône groaned and rocked hard into me, heat spreading as their throbbing cock emptied into my ass.

Rhône collapsed on top of me, my arms and legs wrapping around them.

"That was amazing. You may have to fight me for bottom position from now on," I teased.

"Wouldn't be much of a fight. It's a win-win either way. My cock in you, your cock in me. There are no losers." Rhône sighed into my neck. "We should clean up before we're stuck together forever."

"No losers there either," I joked.

Once we'd showered and climbed back into bed, I pulled Rhône into my arms. "Thank you for that. It was really good. Like, *really* good."

"Yes, it was. Sex is always good. But sex with you is beyond that."

"I don't really like to think of you having sex with others." My chest tightened. "We're committed, right? No sex with others while we're together, right?"

"Of course. I have no desire for anyone else, and I *definitely* don't want to share you with anyone else."

We fell asleep wrapped in each other's arms.

By the time morning came, I hated the thought of leaving Rhône, but I had to get back to work.

Gently extricating myself from their arms, I got ready as quietly as I could. Before I left, I penned a quick love letter and placed it on the bed so they'd find it when they woke up.

Dear Rhône,

Last night was amazing. Thank you. I love you. So damn much. I've been happy and enjoyed relationships with others, but with you it's different. I feel our love in every part of my body. My heart and soul are filled with my love and desire for you. Nothing and no one has ever felt so right. I want you in my arms, in my life, in my body forever. I love you.

Come meet me for lunch today? We can eat out at one of the tables at work.

Can't wait to see you.

Love,

Kellan

NINE

"WHERE THE HELL HAVE YOU BEEN?" Dayne grabbed my arm as I walked across the street toward the DNRP building. The sun peeked from behind the clouds, making the day mild and comfortable.

I yanked myself away. "Um, hello to you, as well." I crossed my arms and frowned.

"I asked where you've been," Dayne shot back.

"No, you rudely demanded," I huffed. "Not cool."

Dayne rolled her eyes. "Sorry." She chewed a nail. "I was just worried. You disappeared for a week. It was like you'd fallen from the face of the earth."

No, just discovered a hidden underground world. Luckily Dayne didn't have the same abilities as Rhône, but I needed to be careful either way. Coming back to the present conversation, I shrugged. "Took the week off."

"A whole week?"

"Yep." I glanced at my phone for the time.

"You've never taken a whole week off work."

"First time for everything. Since I've never done it, I had the days."

"But why? What were you doing? You couldn't even call me?" Dayne pursed her full lips.

"I was spending time with someone. You're not my keeper, I didn't *owe* you a call."

"Someone who?" Dayne's brow pulled into a deep scowl.

"The someone I'm seeing. Look, I need to get to work." I made to walk away, but Dayne grabbed my arm again.

I glanced at her hand on my arm and then at her face. "Stop grabbing me, please."

"Fine, whatever. You used to love my hands on you," Dayne purred.

My patience was wearing thin. "Lots of things I *used* to do."

"So, who are you seeing?" Dayne switched to a cajoling tone. "Is he cute? The sex must be to die for if you took a whole week off work. Is he totally hung?"

I couldn't even try to stop the warm smile that filled my face as I thought about the *who* I'd been seeing. My stomach clenched at Dayne's intrusive questions regarding my sex life though. "Their name is Rhône."

"Rhône? That's weird." Dayne scrunched up her face. "Is he at least cute?"

"*They* are extremely attractive."

"And you spent a whole week with them? Doing what? Where did you stay?" Dayne squinted her eyes.

"I stayed with them and their family," I answered. "And they stayed with me some of the time. What's up with the inquisition?"

"*They*? Why do you keep saying they?"

"Rhône's pronouns are they/them and zie/zir," I explained. "Now, seriously, I need to go. Talk to you later."

"Wait," Dayne called out. "We should hang sometime. Like old times?"

Desperation was *not* a good look for Dayne. I gave a wave and climbed the steps to my building.

———

"AREN'T you going to introduce me?" Dayne's fake-sweet words breathed warmly against my ear and made me want to puke.

Rhône and I were sitting side-by-side at a small covered table outside of the DNRP eating lunch. Anger ignited in my veins. I didn't care for my time with Rhône being interrupted.

"What are you doing here, Dayne?" I asked through gritted teeth.

"Just in the area. Thought I'd see if you wanted to grab lunch, but it appears you've already got a date." Dayne's bottom lip drooped in a fake, pouty smile and batted her lashes.

I reached for Rhône's hand and brought it to my lap. "Dayne, this is Rhône. Rhône, my old friend Dayne."

"Nice to meet you," Rhône murmured and squeezed my hand.

"Likewise, I'm sure," Dayne quipped and blatantly studied Rhône. Her eyes roamed from Rhône's hair, to their clothes, to their sunglasses, before a dangerous sneer filled her face. "Wow, Kel, I guess pansexual means you really go for *all types*. Didn't take you as the type to go for a hermaphrodite."

I shot up from my seat ready to defend Rhône, but they stood beside me, their hand gently rubbing my back. *Do not give in to her ugliness. She's baiting you to get to me. Don't lower yourself. Let me speak.*

"Hermaphrodite is a very old and very derogatory slur, as I'm sure you're well aware. I claim the term intersex. And, as I'm also genderqueer, I use the pronouns they/them and zie/zir. While it's been a...*pleasure*"—Rhône coughed on the word—"meeting you, Kellan and I were having a private lunch before you so rudely interrupted."

Dayne's face burned a fiery shade of red, and she clenched her jaw. "My bad." She turned to me. "She—he?—is a treat, Kel. Looks like you found yourself a real sideshow freak."

"Dayne, shut your mouth," I warned.

Rhône took my hand. "Let it go. She's not worth it."

Dayne spit at our feet before tossing her hair and stalking away.

I took a deep breath and gathered Rhône in my arms. "Oh my God, Rhône, baby, I'm so sorry."

"Did you invite Dayne here? Ask her to speak to me that way?"

"No, never, you've got to know that!"

"Of course, I know that," Rhône assured me. "My point is that you have nothing to apologize for."

"I'm sorry that I ever knew her. I can't believe I was ever involved with someone who could be so ugly and full of hate." I kissed the top of Rhône's head.

As I finished my lunch, I felt a sad, heavy weight sitting on my chest.

"I've got lessons to do the next couple days. But let's meet up in a few days," Rhône suggested. "Maybe dinner with the villagers and then a sleepover at your place?"

I hugged them close. "That sounds amazing."

"Thank you again for the letter. Waking up to it was so special." Rhône kissed me softly. "Waking up with you by my side is better, but if I can't have you, I'll take a love letter every time."

———

I HATED thinking I wouldn't see Rhône for a couple days. I'd gotten so used to having them around; it felt as if part of my heart was missing when they weren't with me.

To keep myself busy while apart, I planned to work

overtime, study up on some paranormal, supernatural, and fantasy books, and deep clean my apartment. Not that I thought I'd *ever* be able to learn all there was to know about the vastness of the otherworldly creatures, but it couldn't hurt to at least try to educate myself. Especially since I was involved with a whole village of extra-sapiens.

I'd just walked through my apartment's door on my first day of no Rhône. My goal was food, then cleaning. But a knock at the door derailed me.

Dayne didn't even wait for me to get the door all the way open before she charged in.

"It's not right, Kellan. That…that *thing* is disgusting. You're trying to tell me you're *attracted* to that? You find some he/she attractive? How can you even think about having sex with whatever that thing is?" Dayne's tirade grew more heated, but her voice faded as I willed myself to remain calm. Closing my eyes, I envisioned the popid fields in the hidden village, the spiritual dance of the elders, the positivity and life of the Popids. She droned on, dragging me back from my musing.

Knowing that Rhône would want me to stay calm, I took a deep breath. "Stop. You're not welcome here if you're going to be hateful about my relationship with Rhône."

"A relationship?? Are you kidding me? Have you even seen what's under those clothes? I mean, you say you're attracted to all kinds of people, but that *thing* isn't right. Like, I can see you liking a male or a female, but a *hermaphrodite?* Oh, I'm sorry, intersex. You can't be okay with that! It's disgusting!" Dayne stood in front of me, spittle flying from her mouth, shaking.

And I knew I'd lost her. Or she'd lost me. I could never, *ever*, be friends with someone so full of hate.

"You need to go."

"Where is the he/she even from?" Dayne demanded.

"None of your business."

"You're making a mistake, Kel. You are too messed up to see it now, but one day you'll see it, and you'll be glad I was here to warn you."

"Leave. Stay away from me. Stay away from Rhône."

"That thing doesn't deserve you. I'm sorry, but it doesn't."

I closed my eyes, clenched my teeth, and took a deep breath before slamming my hand against the door. "You need to leave. *Now.* Before I call the police."

"This isn't over," Dayne threatened.

"It is. We're over. I don't want your hate anywhere near me."

Dayne shook her head, nostrils flaring. "You'll see, this isn't over. And then you'll be sorry."

I slammed the door shut behind her and spent the next twenty minutes trying to calm myself.

My phone buzzed, and I opened a text from Rhône.

Don't let her hate win.

Have some tea. Read, clean, take a shower, just try to relax.

I love you.

I took a deep breath and replied to Rhône that I'd do my best.

Two hours later, my apartment was spotless, and I was cuddled in bed with popid tea and a book about magic. I sighed and smiled. As angry as I'd been earlier, Rhône's words had helped to calm me. I purposefully sent my thoughts out in hopes of Rhône picking up on them.

Within seconds, Rhône's words filled my head.

Glad you're feeling better.

See you day after tomorrow.

Love you.

Rhône was so good at hearing the words I sent their way. I was even getting better at sending them. I knew I was improving at hearing Rhône's thoughts, but I wanted to be able to do it without Rhône purposefully sending thoughts my way. Maybe zie would work with me on that. They and their parents swore up and down that I had *something special,* so maybe, with help, I could make it happen.

———

Rhône

I felt her presence before I saw her.

Dayne.

Strengthen the wards. I sent my thoughts to the Popids in hopes they could protect the village. I knew my responsibility would be to draw Dayne away from the area. I could *not* let her see the waterfall if the wards and charms were to weaken.

I turned away from the hidden entrance to the village and headed toward the park.

Dayne quickened her pace and cut me off.

"Rhône, hi. Didn't expect to see you here."

Funny, you followed me here, why wouldn't you expect to see me?

"Dayne, nice to see you," I lied.

"You live around here?" Dayne stood with her arms crossed, a frown distorting her face.

"Just thought I'd come enjoy the park for a while," I evaded her question.

"You don't deserve him, you know that, right?"

"Kellan isn't a prize to be won. He's free to make his choice of partner, and for now, he's chosen me." I took a deep breath, pulling strength from Mother Earth as I ran my thumb over the muscovite crystal in my pocket.

"You're some sort of freak of nature, some paranormal creature. I just know it. Kellan went on and on about seeing someone at a waterfall and hidden cave. I thought he was trippin', but I bet it was you. He swore the disappearing waterfall was around here, right in this area." Dayne narrowed her eyes as she studied me, watching for anything that would give her information.

Oh, my sweet Kellan. He would be so upset if he realized trusting his friend put the village in danger.

"He only ever talked about the mystery person and

waterfall that one time, but I'd swear on my next fix that it was you he meant, and the precious waterfall is around here somewhere."

"I'm unclear as to what you're speaking of. But I should really be going." I tried to sidestep Dayne.

Her hand shot out and yanked my arm, hard.

I winced and bit back a cry of pain.

Kellan. I'm in trouble. I need to protect the village, but I'm worried Dayne is out to harm me, the Popids, everything.

Would Kellan be able to hear me? I truly believed he had the ability, but we'd not yet worked to perfectly hone his skills.

"Please unhand me," I demanded through gritted teeth.

"You disgust me. You're a freak. People like you shouldn't be allowed to exist." Dayne let go of my arm with a strong push, and I nearly fell backward. "What's your power? Aside from having two holes and a cock for some kinky sex, what's so special about you? What did you do to Kellan to hook him?"

"Dayne, I am an intersex individual. That is all. Kellan is attracted to me all on his own. I'd like to end this conversation now." Again, I tried to leave.

"Don't think so, freak. Here's the deal. I've got a super powerful boss who wants information about you, your people—assuming you're not the only freak living behind some invisible waterfall—and your home. My boss also wants you as far away from Kellan as possible.

I'm totally on board with that part. So, we can do this the easy way or the hard way."

My mind raced. Who would want Kellan away from me? I couldn't allow Dayne to find the village. I *had* to draw her away from the area.

"Shall we go to the park and discuss the situation?" I suggested.

Dayne threw her head back and laughed. "Don't think so, freakshow. You're going to take me to where you live and give me some sort of info to share with the boss."

Popids were a peaceful people. We thrived on peace and goodness and positivity. We were committed to not using our magic to control people, not harming others with our powers, only using our magic for good.

One could argue magicking Dayne away from the village entrance was controlling her. But one could also argue it was for the overall good of the Popids. I needed a moment to gather my thoughts and make my decision.

Unfortunately, I didn't get that moment. In a split second, Dayne made the decision for me.

I fell hard to the ground, pain reverberating through my body.

Dayne was over me, sneering, hate spewing from her mouth.

The pain and suddenness of the attack weakened my powers to the point all I could do was curl into a ball and attempt to protect myself.

The white-hot pain of Dayne's fists and shoes pummeling me soon eased to a heavy blackness. All thoughts and recognition faded to oblivion.

Kellan.

He was my last coherent thought before all went dark.

TEN

THE DAY after I cleaned my apartment and threw out Dayne, I took a sick day from work. I could count on one hand the times I'd taken a sick day. But about an hour before I was to start my shift, I was hit with the worst headache and pain in my stomach I'd ever had. It was as if my head was being beaten by a baseball bat and my stomach was being punched repeatedly. I could barely breathe and found myself curled in a fetal position on my bed. My entire body hurt.

I made it through calling in my sick day before vomiting in the kitchen sink. Throwing up made my head feel as if it would split in two. I took a large dose of ibuprofen and quickly heated water for tea. Definitely not *proper* tea, but I hoped the popid leaves would ease some of my pain.

By the time the tea was ready, I could barely walk upright to my bed. I forced myself to drink the entire mug and huddled under a blanket, before I succumbed to the pain and exhaustion. All I wanted to do, all I felt physically capable of doing, was to fall into a deep sleep. Maybe resting would ease the pain.

I woke several hours later groggy and disoriented. The explosive pain in my head and stomach had eased to deep, throbbing aches, which traveled through my entire body. I fumbled for my phone, finally finding it under the comforter I held around my shivering body. Dead. I whimpered. Calling Rhône seemed important. They would want to know I was sick. Maybe they already sensed it? But zie needed to stay away. What if I was contagious? Could Popids get outer world germs and sicknesses? It was a question I'd never thought to ask.

My aching body revolted at the thought of crawling from bed to find my phone charger. I'd have to build up the strength and conviction to move first. I fell asleep with the goal of charging my phone when I awakened.

But the next time I woke up, my eyes felt as if they were swollen shut and my torso hurt so badly I could barely take a full breath. My apartment was dark. The thought of moving from bed, turning on a light, trying to eat, all of it made me hurt all over. I gently moved to a somewhat more comfortable position and fell back to sleep.

Kellan.

I woke with a start. How long had I slept this time?

Light was streaming through my windows, and my eyes burned from the brightness.

I glanced around the apartment. Rhône had called my name, but I didn't see them.

Doing a quick assessment of my body, I determined that I was still in pain, but it appeared I'd live. I wasn't hungry, but I wanted a drink. I knew I needed to hydrate. I'd been asleep well over twelve hours and barely needed to take a piss. I was well on my way to dehydration if not already there.

I rolled from the bed and stood, hunched and trembling, until the dizziness faded. Knowing I had a limited time before I'd need to be back in bed, I shuffled to the kitchen to start water for tea. After another handful of ibuprofen, along with an apology to my liver, I then headed to the bathroom. I peed, washed my face, and gripped my phone charger like I'd won a prize.

By the time I poured the water over the popid tea, I realized I had only a few minutes of strength left before collapsing. I grabbed crackers and my mug of still-steeping tea and dragged myself back to bed. Breathing heavily, I struggled to plug the charger into the wall before connecting it to my phone.

My plan was crackers, tea, and a little rest while the phone charged. Then I'd call Rhône. I was sure they had blown my phone up with texts and calls worrying about me. My heart hurt a little that they hadn't come to check on me, but maybe Rhône sensed my sickness and stayed away because of that. I managed three crackers and most of the tea before rolling to my side, trying to take a deep breath, and holding my aching ribs and abdomen as I slipped back into a fitful sleep.

I woke later, still in pain and exhausted, but anxious to contact Rhône.

Picking up my now charged phone, I was confused and slightly annoyed—or maybe I was disappointed—that Rhône hadn't called or texted even once. We hadn't gone over twenty-four hours without communicating in, well, the whole time I'd known them. Was Rhône angry I hadn't reached out? That wasn't like them, but maybe that's what had happened. I tapped out a text.

Sorry I went dark. I've been so sick. Started yesterday. Not AS bad today, but still feel terrible. Hoping to be better by tomorrow so we can still meet up. Going to sleep some more. Text or call. Love you.

I slept for about two hours.

Rhône hadn't texted or called.

By this time, I was miffed, but I also had the beginnings of serious worries.

Rhône wasn't the type to ignore out of anger. They were always likely to talk things out.

So that meant Rhône hadn't reached out to me in well over twenty-four hours, closer to thirty-six. Something was wrong. I needed to contact them. I thumbed the phone and made a call.

No answer on Rhône's phone.

Something was definitely wrong.

I needed to get out of bed and get to the village. My

head may as well have been a melon dropped and busted on the ground. I almost expected it to be oozing. I could barely stand up straight. Breathing was painful. And my stomach threatened to turn on me at any moment.

But I had to get to Rhône.

Rhône, I'm coming to you. Don't worry. Just wait for me.

I REACHED the area where the waterfall would be if it was visible.

My heart sank and soared.

The waterfall wasn't there. That was good. The village was safe.

The waterfall wasn't there. That was bad. I couldn't get ahold of Rhône and had no way of getting into the village.

I huddled onto a park bench in front of the waterfall location.

An hour later, after continuous calls to Rhône's phone and making my head hurt even worse trying to send thoughts their way, I gave up and dragged myself home.

After a painful and restless night of sleep, I pulled myself from bed and headed to the park once again. The waterfall still wasn't there.

While I kept wanting to convince myself that it was *good* I couldn't see the waterfall, my heart told me something was very wrong. But I was stuck. I couldn't get to the village. I couldn't contact Rhône. I had no idea how to contact Nayel or Rube. My body hurt. My heart hurt.

With one last look over my shoulder, and one last useless call to Rhône, I left the area and headed to the only place I knew I could possibly find help.

———

"DR. WINSTON WILL SEE YOU NOW," the front desk assistant, Katarina, smiled and gestured toward Maeve's door.

I rushed into Dr. Winston's office as quickly as my pained body would allow.

"Kellan, what's wrong, child?" Maeve instantly bustled around her desk and hurried me into a chair as she felt my forehead. She pulled her hand back, hissing in pain. "You are hurt."

"I'm hurt, but it's better than it was. Something is wrong with the Popids."

"Did someone do this to you?"

"No, I just got sick at my apartment. Felt like I was being beaten to a pulp, seriously thought I was dying." I shifted gently in the chair. "But I've lost all contact with Rhône, and I can't see the waterfall."

Maeve peered at me, eyes squinted and lips pursed, before heading back to her side of the desk. "It's good that you can't see the waterfall."

"I know that, but Rhône hasn't contacted me in two days, and I can't get ahold of them. We were in constant contact, and we had plans to meet up. Something is wrong."

Maeve's brows gave away her surprise. "So, you're in a relationship with Rhône? Do you feel that's a wise decision?"

I couldn't stop the smile that filled my face as I nodded. "Yeah. They are amazing. I've met their parents and the villagers and all that."

Maeve seemed impressed. "Popids allowing you into the village is quite unusual. They must see the same special something in you that I do."

I shrugged. "So, they keep saying. But it's not usual for Rhône to cut off contact. My gut tells me something is wrong." My eyes stung with tears, and my stomach churned with fear. "I need your help. I didn't know where else to turn."

"What could I possibly do?"

"I don't know, use your powers or something to contact the village and have them let me in?" I clasped my hands together, knuckles white.

"Using my powers to contact the village on behalf of a lovestruck man would be highly unusual and very much out of compliance. This is not an emergency."

"It very much *could be* an emergency!" I exploded.

Maeve was silent for several moments, eyes squinted as she studied me.

"If I were to contact the village, I would need your

word that you are only concerned about the Popids' well-being and checking on Rhône, nothing more."

My face pulled into a frown. "Why else would I be wanting to get to the village?"

Maeve pressed her lips together. "The village has many enemies."

I knew my wide eyes bordered on disrespectful. "Sure, there are assholes who want to hurt them, study them, demolish them, and use them, but I'm *not* one of those people!"

"Calm down. I didn't mean to insinuate you were. It's just not often that I see a non-extra-sapien showing such interest in the extra-sapien world without having some sort of harmful or self-profiting agenda."

Her words stung, but I pushed aside my feelings because it was more important to find out about Rhône and the village. "I just need to know that Rhône's okay."

"What if their parents or a villager says Rhône is fine but doesn't want to see you?"

My heart stuttered. Would that happen? Had Rhône decided they didn't want to see me? No. I knew in my heart that something was wrong and Rhône needed me. Maybe they didn't *need* me, but Rhône was in trouble or hurting. Or both.

I swallowed and shook my head. "That won't happen."

"You don't know that. Maybe your relationship was more one-sided than you realized."

"If I hear from Rhône that they don't want to see me, I will accept it." Like hell I'd accept it. A relationship like the one I had with Rhône wasn't one that could just be dropped and forgotten.

Maeve cleared her throat and rolled her eyes.

Shit. That mind reading crap was annoying as hell.

She smirked.

"Please?" I was at the end of my rope, I had no clue what else to do.

Maeve pulled a cellular phone from her desk and thumbed the screen.

"What are you doing?"

"Calling the Popids."

"You have their number?"

"Don't you have Rhône's number?" Maeve asked.

"Well, yeah, but I didn't realize *you* had a direct line to the village."

"I'm the head of Department of Paranormal, Supernatural, and Fantasy Science. I have contact information for beings, creatures, and entities you've never even imagined." Maeve turned her attention to the phone call. "Hello, yes, this is Dr. Maeve Winston. I have Kellan Roberts here with me. He would like to get a message to Popid Rhône. May I leave his number?"

I grabbed a piece of paper and scratched my number on it. If Rhône's phone was dead or broken, Nayel and Rube would have had no way of knowing my number.

"Yes, please tell Rhône that Kellan is worried about zir. He would like Rhône to contact him if possible."

Maeve then rattled off Kellan's number before saying thank you and hanging up.

"Thank you." I breathed a sigh of relief.

"That's as far as I'm willing to go. If you do not hear from the Popids, you must let this infatuation go."

"I understand. Thank you." I stood to leave.

Maeve spoke, causing me to pause by the door. "Relationships between humans and extra-sapiens often don't work. While I do understand the draw on both sides, it almost always turns out a failure."

I pressed my lips together. "Almost always. Means Rhône and I could be the ones proving it wrong." *Proving you wrong* ran through my head, but I nodded and gave a small wave goodbye, making my way out the door before I could see if Maeve read what I was thinking.

I checked my phone. It was completely charged. I headed to work. Despite not wanting to be there, I needed the distraction and the money. I turned my ringer on and prayed for a phone call from the village.

ELEVEN

THE PHONE CALL didn't come that day.

Or the next.

I was crazy with worry, but I schlepped through my shifts the best I could.

I couldn't go back to Maeve.

Dayne was MIA, and I didn't really want to talk to her at all.

I found myself at my parents' home one evening with no real purpose other than desiring their comfort.

"Kellan, what a nice surprise. Come in, come in. Your mother is in the kitchen." Dad pulled me into a hug before leading me away from the door.

"Oh, my goodness. I'm so happy to see you." Mom dried her hands on a towel before wrapping me in a warm embrace in the middle of their comfortable and well-used kitchen.

The pain and worry of the last few days bubbled

from deep inside, and I found myself sobbing on my mother's shoulder.

"Kellan, baby boy, what's wrong?" Mom rubbed my back and let me cry. "Turn that soup down to simmer," she ordered my dad. "We'll sit in the family room, and you can tell us all about it."

I sat curled up in the corner of the old worn couch with Mom at the other end, and Dad settled onto the recliner. "Remember I told you about meeting someone?" I didn't wait for them to acknowledge the memory. "Rhône is amazing, and we are completely in love. But something has happened, and they've been cut off from me completely. We were seeing each other almost daily, and then one day we were supposed to meet, and they never showed up. I can't get ahold of them on the phone."

Dad cleared his throat. "Maybe Rhône needed a break? Too much too soon?"

"Have you tried going to their home to check on them?" Mom suggested.

I took a deep breath. "So, here's the thing. Rhône isn't one hundred percent human."

Mom's eyes widened.

"Okay, Rhône isn't human. They are a Popid. They live in a hidden underground village."

Mom and Dad didn't laugh or gasp like I'd expected. They simply made eye contact over my head and seemed to have their own conversation.

"I've heard of the Popids before. I was never sure if

they were real or just folklore." Dad spoke from his
chair behind me.

I turned so that I could see both of my parents.
"Popids are very real. I've been to their village. I've met
Rhône's parents. I've seen the popid fields. I've met the
village elders and eaten dinner there." Pulling my knees
to my chest, I let the tears fall. "And I'm so scared
something is wrong with Rhône. It's completely unlike
them to cut communication like this."

After explaining more about why I couldn't just go
to Rhône's house or contact their parents, I found
myself exhausted. "Can I just sleep here tonight?"

"Of course, you can." Mom stood. "I'll make up the
bed in your old room. But first, you need to eat. And
you can plug your phone in on the kitchen counter to
charge it up. If your Rhône calls, you want to be sure to
get it."

By the time dinner was done, my bones were heavy
weights dragging my body down. I needed to sleep; my
body was still recovering from being ill. I needed to
hear from Rhône. At this point, I was willing to give zir
whatever space they needed just to know they were safe
and healthy.

I gave both my parents a hug and trudged up the
old, worn staircase. My hot shower was as quick as
possible in case the phone rang. My head and heart
battled over whether I should just accept I'd lost Rhône
forever.

The next morning, I awoke to the shrill chirp of my

phone. Fumbling to pick it up, I squinted at the UNKNOWN on the screen.

"Hello?" I barked into the phone almost before I even had it to my ear. "Rhône?"

"Kellan, it's Nayel."

"Where's Rhône? Are they okay? Please, I just need to know zie is okay." My eyes stung with unshed tears.

"Kellan, we need you to come to the village. All will be explained then."

"Tell me if they are okay."

"Have you felt your connection with Rhône fade?"

I faltered at the question.

"What?"

"You and Rhône had a connection. Did it ever seem to dim or fade away?"

When I stopped to think about it, I realized Nayel was right. My heart warmed. "No, it never went away." I hadn't heard Rhône's thoughts, but my heart and soul still felt a strong connection to Rhône.

"Then you should know Rhône is okay. Battered and bruised, but it takes more than that to destroy a Popid." Nayel paused for the briefest of moments. "But it is of utmost importance that you come to the village."

"Of course. I can be at the park in thirty minutes. Will Rhône be meeting me?" I jumped from bed and began to dress.

"A villager will be there to meet you and escort you." Nayel disconnected.

Shoving my feet into shoes, I sprinted down the stairs.

"Whoa, where's the fire?" Dad glanced up from his coffee.

"It's Rhône. Their parents called. I'm going to meet them."

Mom handed me a glass of juice. "Drink this. You need something in your stomach."

I drained the juice before hugging her. "Thanks. Thank you both for listening to me last night."

"Be careful. And let Rhône know we'd very much like to meet...*them*." Mom stumbled over the words, but my heart soared that she was trying.

"I will. Soon, I promise."

I bolted from the house and ran toward the park.

———

I PACED the sidewalk for several moments before realizing I may call attention to myself, so I sat on the bench and stared at the waterfall's general area. Could I will Rhône to appear?

"Rhône isn't well enough to meet you. But if you'll come with me, I'll be sure to get you safely into the village." The voice from behind startled me.

I jumped from my seat, and turned toward the speaker. Popid Ximon? They were one of the most powerful Popids in the village, very private and quiet, but they seemed kind. "Were you sent to lead me?"

"Yes, of course. Let's go."

My phone buzzed with a text.

Nayel.

I'm coming to the surface. Are you there yet?

My heart stuttered in suspicion. Wasn't Ximon already here to lead me to the village? Why was Ximon here if Nayel was coming to get me? I glanced up from my phone and Ximon was gone. Simply vanished. What the hell?

"Kellan?" Nayel appeared beside me. "What's wrong? You look as if you've seen a ghost."

"Ximon was here. Told me Rhône wasn't well enough to meet me and that they would lead me to the village." I looked around the space where the person had been. "But then you texted, and they disappeared. Not like walked away. Completely disappeared in a split second."

Nayel frowned. "There is much to tell you. Come." Rhône's parent took my hand, and we walked toward the hidden falls.

A cool, wet mist clung to my skin as we passed through the water, and before I knew it, we were in the cave heading down the stairs.

"That will never not be amazingly cool."

Nayel laughed.

"Is Rhône sick?"

"Rhône is resting and healing. Zie has been asking for you during their lucid moments."

We reached the village, and I was met with many

friendly faces and greetings. Rube pulled me into a hug, and I knew I was as at home here with the Popids as I was when I was in the presence of my own parents.

"Please come. We will sit with Rhône while Rube and I fill you in on what has happened and what we know." Nayel gestured toward Rhône's room.

Rhône appeared small and fragile in their bed.

I rushed to zir side and took their hand. "Rhône, baby. What happened?"

Turning to Rhône's parents, I asked. "Can they hear me? Are they just sleeping or more?"

Rube rubbed my shoulder. "Rhône is medicated to allow for deep sleep. They have been awake more and more lately, but we're keeping them as sedated as possible for the best healing. We will let the popid wear off so they will soon be coherent."

Nayel and Rube pulled chairs close to Rhône's bed as if they knew I would not leave their side.

"What happened?" I asked again, and a crushing weight took my breath as I knew without a doubt that I wasn't going to like the answer. I glanced up from Rhône's hand in mine. "I have a feeling today is going to change everything."

Nayel and Rube, lips pressed in twin looks of dismay, looked first at each other and then to me. "Change is inevitable," Rube whispered.

"But why do I get the feeling that whatever you're going to tell me is going to be a very painful change?" I rubbed my chest as if to soothe my heart. A new understanding zinged through my blood. "And danger. I feel danger."

"Change is often painful or at least uncomfortable," Rube stated. "Danger is unfortunately something the Popids face all too often."

"Get comfortable. I'm calling for food and drink, and then Rube and I will tell you what we know. There's a vast amount of information for us to share and for you to process. You will need to keep up your strength." Nayel stepped from the room.

I climbed onto the bed and pulled Rhône into my arms as Rube stood and blanketed us both with the comforter. Rhône stirred and curled into my body. Never had I known such beautiful, perfect fulfillment, even as my heart hurt and urged me to prepare for danger.

Nayel returned, followed by a Popid carrying a tray of food and drinks.

"Drink the popid juice first. It will allow you to relax and hear our words." Nayel handed me a small cup of pure purple juice.

I downed the juice, the effects immediately coursing through my body. I nodded. "I'm ready."

Nayel took a seat and reached for Rube's hand.

"We will begin with what happened to Rhône because we know it is your utmost concern. However, we must ask that you not disturb Rhône with negativity or anger as hard as that might be." Nayel raised a brow and waited for my response.

"Agreed. I wouldn't hurt Rhône in any way."

"Rhône was beaten by a woman named Dayne," Rube began. "I believe you know her?"

My stomach clenched, and I had to bite my tongue to keep from releasing the stream of obscenities begging to escape. Instead, I simply nodded, my jaw locked and nostrils flaring, the metallic taste of blood coating my mouth.

"Dayne hurt Rhône very badly. Because of this, and also because we are more sure than ever that a traitor is among us, the waterfall appeared. Dayne knew to look for it, we believe, because she'd heard you speak of it. But it also appears Dayne was told of the Popid village by someone else. Someone with evil intent. Because no other human has seen the waterfall, and as it doesn't appear that Dayne has *any* extra-sapien blood, we believe someone may have charmed her to be able to see the waterfall."

The popid juice threatened to come back up. Dayne knew about the waterfall because of me. Rhône got hurt because of me.

"Kellan, don't think that way. Rhône would never blame you, and neither do we."

No. Don't think that. Rhône's thoughts comforted me only slightly more than Nayel and Rube's insistence that I was not at fault.

"Once behind the waterfall, Dayne was able to enter the cave and gain access to the village because she had Rhône with her." Nayel shifted in the chair, never letting go of Rube's hand. "The village had already felt the evil and negativity when Dayne attacked our child. We were working hard to strengthen the wards on the waterfall and cave. But when Dayne entered the village, our instincts were on high alert. We had to divide and conquer. The majority of the village worked to tighten our magic and send positivity to our Mother Earth, or else our entire existence was in danger. Our precious Rhône was immediately taken to the popid fields where zie remained in a healing state with round-the-clock treatment and care. Our strongest members apprehended and detained Dayne and set to work interrogating her; she spoke only of a powerful boss. A struggle ensued as Dayne was very angry, and the village worked to neutralize her."

"Why didn't anyone contact me? I was sick with worry." Comprehension suddenly dawned on me. "I felt the attack," I gasped and fought the acid roiling in my stomach. "Oh my God, I felt the beating. I thought I was just super sick. But my head and stomach felt as if they were being beaten to a pulp. I felt what Rhône felt."

"Kellan, we would have contacted you immediately, but there were extenuating circumstances."

"What? What could have possibly kept you from making sure I was here with Rhône to help them heal?"

"The simplest answer is that Rhône's phone was busted, completely useless, and we realized quickly that we'd never exchanged numbers with you, so we faced an obstacle." Nayel squeezed Rube's hand.

"An obstacle that your powers could have easily overcome," I accused. "What are you not telling me?" While hearing about Rhône's attack had been painful, I felt it to my core that more was coming.

"I'm sorry, Kellan, we *had* to be sure you weren't part of what Dayne did to Rhône."

I jerked back as if I'd been slapped. "How could you even think that?"

"You were once involved with Dayne, correct?"

"Yes, but that was in the past, and I would *never.*" My nostrils flared. "You invited me into the village, you trusted me, you made me one of your own. How could you think I'd be part of Dayne hurting Rhône?" My voice cracked, and my eyes stung with tears.

"You have to understand, we didn't want to question you. But we already have a traitor we've not been able to uncover. Forgive us, but we had to clear your name before we allowed you back into the village."

Rhône stirred against my side, their eyes fluttering open.

"We will take a break. Visit with each other for a while. When you both feel up to it, we'll continue with the telling." Rube stood and pulled Nayel to stand by their side. "You will need each other's strength in the coming days. Turn to each other, lean on each other, strengthen the bonds you've built." Rube patted my shoulder and then followed Nayel from the room.

"KELLAN, YOU'RE HERE," Rhône whispered.

"I've been trying to be here for days, but couldn't contact anyone." I kissed their head and held them tightly. "I'm so sorry. I can't help but feel this is all my fault. Dayne knew about you because of me."

"Yes, but it appears to be more in-depth than that." Rhône shifted. "I'll tell you, but I need you to do something for me first."

"What? Anything," I assured.

"Kiss me. Please?"

With zero hesitation, I bent and took Rhône's lips. The electric current between us was faint, but it was there. And it increased as the kiss deepened. I pulled away, but only a fraction. "There will *never* be a time when kissing you is a chore. Don't ever think that."

Rhône sighed against my lips and seemed to be content to just breathe me in for several moments.

"Are you okay?" I ran a hand up and down Rhône's arm.

"I'm still tired, but I've been healing."

"Do you hurt?"

"A little, but it's getting better each day." Rhône nuzzled into my hand. "Go ahead. I know you have questions."

"Dayne spoke of a powerful boss. Someone who had sent her to infiltrate and gather information. And that boss specifically wanted me far away from you. And the boss, or someone in the extra-sapien community, charmed Dayne to be able to see the waterfall. I know people want to learn about the Popids. And some who want to destroy the Popids because of their differences and their powers." I frowned. "But who would want me away from you?"

"I don't know. I believe we've been questioning Dayne for that information, but so far she hasn't budged."

"I need to see her." I stood from the bed. "Maybe she'll talk to me."

"You'll need me to grant entrance and access to the prisoner." Rhône shuddered and allowed me to help them from the bed. "Holding prisoners is not the way of the Popids. It brings sadness and negativity."

I took Rhône's hand, and we shuffled slowly toward the area where Dayne was being kept. Rhône spoke to the guards and then ushered me inside.

"I will stay out here." Rhône gestured at the open space outside of a second closed door. "Dayne's negativity is not good for my healing. You may question her. I can watch on the camera and, of course, hear your thoughts. Don't get too close to her. Dayne is desperate and dangerous. Our empaths have been delving into her thoughts. Although the remains of some sort of drug are blocking her mind somewhat. We've still been able to gather that her *boss* is paying a very large sum of money, or offering drugs, and Dayne would likely do anything to make sure she gets that money, or the drugs, or both."

Rhône unlocked the second door, leaving it somewhat opened behind me. I found myself in a dark room with only the dimmest of lights on the rock walls. Half of the room was furnished with a desk, chairs, a small refrigerator, and a couch. Dayne's half of the room was behind bars and contained only a cot and a toilet.

"Kellan, thank God you're here," Dayne exclaimed and clamored from her cot to cling to the bars. "You've got to get me out of here. These freaks have kept me locked up like an animal."

She's been well fed and hydrated. She's been allowed to wash and given clean clothes daily.

Rhône's words filled my mind, and I smirked. "Nice try, Dayne. But you and I both know you've likely got it better in this cage than you ever did on your own."

Dayne spit in my direction. "So, it's too late? They've brainwashed you?"

"No, I just know the facts. But I do question who has brainwashed *you*."

"Kellan, I have to get out of here, please," Dayne begged. "My boss gave me a time limit. I have to get out so I can get my money."

"Who is your boss?" I demanded. "And what could they possibly pay you for? You have no information to give."

"Unless you're getting me out of here, I have no reason to tell you who I'm working for." Dayne laid down the gauntlet. Her self-righteous face sneering between the bars.

I wanted to hurt her, to punish her for what she'd done to Rhône. Yet I stood my ground, arms crossed over my chest.

Hurting her would only bring pain and harm to the village. Rhône threw their thoughts my way.

Well, I may not be able to help myself from knocking her smug ass down a few notches. I heard Rhône laugh as they heard my thoughts.

"Well, well, is that your freakshow out there?" Dayne drawled.

"You don't get to talk about them. Shut up."

"What's the sex like? Must be all kinds of kinky, huh?"

"Shut up."

"It has to be amazing. That's the only way I can see you being able to stomach a freak like that."

"I won't tell you again, Dayne. Shut. Up."

"How many holes does she have? Or do you like to pretend it's a *he* when you're fucking his ass? Do you fuck her in the...?"

Dayne flew through the air and slammed into the solid rock wall of the cave before she could finish her obscene questions.

"I said, *shut up!*" I knew immediately that I'd somehow thrown Dayne against that wall. I didn't know *how*, but I knew my anger, and my love for Rhône had allowed me that power. My hands shook, and my chest felt tight. *I did that. I sent Dayne flying through the air.*

Kellan, you should leave now. Rhône's soft thoughts calmed me.

Two Popids entered the room to tend to Dayne, and I left with my jaw clenched.

Nayel and Rube were with Rhône.

"That was impressive," Nayel commented. "Did you mean to throw her like that?"

"No, it just happened. I mean"—I hung my head—"I wanted to hurt her, to shut her up, but I didn't *try* to fling her against the wall. I'm sorry. I know my thoughts and actions were negative." I swallowed hard.

Rube took my hand and placed a muscovite crystal about the size of a deck of cards on my palm while Rhône put a necklace of muscovite crystal around my neck. My body hummed with warm energy and the shock and awe I felt calmed immediately.

"These crystals will allow you to harness your powers. Your skills are very unrefined and immature. It will take years for you to hone and perfect your powers. However, you appear to have an amazing strength, which baffles us. Keep the crystals on your body at all times." Rube closed my hand around the muscovite.

"So, you think I was able to throw Dayne against the wall like that? And I could do it again? I don't know, I think it was because I was so angry. I think my energy just exploded. I don't know that I could do it again."

"Let's go to the popid fields. Young Kellan can

practice some basics." Nayel gestured toward the door, and we left the holding area. "I fear it would be best if Kellan had some control of his newly discovered powers. And soon. More danger is on its way."

"That's not comforting," I stated. But I knew Nayel was right. I could feel something bad looming on the horizon, as well.

TWELVE

OUR LITTLE GROUP trooped to the fields.

"You ready for this?" Rhône asked. They were obviously tired, but excitement and support for me hummed around them.

"Define ready," I huffed. "I'm getting ready to train in order to hone my powers. Powers I've been told my whole life I don't have." *Holy shit! My powers! I had fucking powers.* "So, if ready means excited, anxious, determined, and nervous as fuck, then yes, I'm ready."

Rhône smiled and rested their head on my shoulder. "You'll be amazing. I've known it since we met, and I believe it even more now."

Rhône relaxed and healed in the popid fields while Nayel and Rube taught me the basics of controlling my powers. Hearing the thoughts of others was easiest if I was calm, focused, and listening for the voice. But I found the stronger the person sending their thoughts, the easier it was to hear them. So, hearing Rhône and their parents was pretty simple once I mastered what I was listening for.

Using the muscovite crystal wasn't as easy.

"It appears you're able to push away an enemy, so for now, let's focus on that. We can work up to other skills." Nayel stood before me as if ready for battle.

"Kellan, we'll start with only the crystal. Keep it in your hand, wield it as a weapon toward your enemies, harnessing your power to explode from the crystal."

I chuckled nervously. "I have absolutely no clue how to do that."

"Can you picture it in your mind? Focus your anger and your energy, push it from deep within to burst from the muscovite." Rube stood next to me and lifted my right arm, the one holding the crystal, and showed me how to hold it. "Try to push Nayel backward."

"But Nayel isn't my enemy. I have no anger toward them."

"Close your eyes. Imagine your anger toward Dayne. Push all of that anger from the inside, picture it flowing from the crystal and pushing Dayne away."

I closed my eyes. Harnessing every bit of anger I had toward Dayne, I imagined all of it shooting from the crystal toward Dayne. The muscovite around my neck heated against my skin. A surge of warmth and energy hummed through my body as a current shot from the crystal in my hand to knock Nayel down. "Whoa! Nayel, I'm sorry." I rushed to help them up.

"Don't be, child. That was impressive. Imagine what you will do with practice."

Rhône's words filtered into my mind. *Wonderful. I told you there was something in you.*

I glanced Rhône's way and couldn't stop the grin from spreading across my face. "So, you think I have powers." I paused when I caught Nayel's raised a brow. "Okay, okay, I *have* powers." I ran a hand over my face and took a deep breath trying to calm my excitement. "Why do I need a muscovite to harness them and you don't?"

"There is so much still to tell you, but suffice it to say that your powers appear to be from a combination of sources. And using the crystal isn't a hindrance. In fact, Rube and I feel that you will one day be more powerful than many of the villagers." Nayel put an arm around Rube's shoulders.

"What?" My jaw dropped. "No way. Even with years of practicing, all I can do is knock someone over and hear some thoughts. I could never be as powerful as a Popid. I have no skills in spells, wards, or charms."

Nayel and Rube smiled slyly.

When are you going to learn to listen to my parents and me when we say you've got powers? Rhône smiled when I met their eyes behind Nayel and Rube.

"Fine." I held up my hands in defeat. "I don't see how it can be that way, but I believe you."

"Good," Nayel stated with a final nod.

"Wow, no way did I ever think I'd be anything close

to a Popid." I took a deep breath and sighed heavily. It was a lot to take in. "I need to practice more, but I don't want to keep knocking over Nayel."

"Stay here by the fields. Rhône can rest, and you can gather popid energy while you practice. We'll have some of the sparring dummies brought out." Rube gestured toward the chair where Rhône was sitting with their feet in the popids.

An hour later, I had quite quickly and successfully managed to hone the power of knocking my enemies away as evidenced by the sparring dummies knocked down and spread out along the ground. The more I used the skill, the easier it got, and the better I was able to control it.

"I wish I could learn everything all at once," I told Rhône. "And I want so badly to make your parents tell me all they know about my powers." I huffed, impatient to know everything.

Before Rhône could answer, alarms sounded in the village.

Rhône shot from their chair and grabbed my arm. "Something is wrong."

Nayel and Rube rushed to the fields.

"Kellan, there is much to tell you, but we must protect the village first." Nayel gripped my shoulders. "Rely *only* on your connection to Rhône and us. Trust your heart, but trust no one else. We fear that those you know may not be exactly what they appear."

A loud and fear-filled commotion sounded.

"Rhône, keep Kellan with you at all times," Rube ordered. "If the danger gets to be too much, retreat to the safe room. The children and a couple keepers are already there. We will split into two groups. One will fend off the danger; the second will strengthen the wards, increase charms of protection, and send positive vibes to our Mother Earth."

"Kellan and I will fend off danger, he's not ready to work with charms or wards yet." Rhône took hold of my hand.

"They're right. I'm totally not." I squeezed Rhône's hand. "But I'd like to point out I'm also not ready to fend off danger either."

"The safe room is an option if you get overwhelmed."

Rube and Nayel ran to man their stations.

"What's the danger?" I asked, afraid of the answer.

Rhône was quiet, eyes closed. They breathed in deeply. "Intruders. Many intruders. Some here for Dayne, some for more intrusive and harmful reasons." Rhône gripped my hand tightly. "Kellan, it's imperative that you trust no one. Things are not always what they seem. Listen to me and to your heart."

"Easy," I quipped. "You *are* my heart."

"Then let's go." Rhône kissed me quickly before we headed to defend the village.

———

WE ROUNDED the corner to find a large number of Popids facing off against a team of approximately ten outerworld police officers. One of our Popid elders stepped forward, hands held out, palms up in a gesture of peace.

One of our *Popid elders?* Rhône's words filtered into my head.

My heart swelled and I could only smile. *Yeah, one of ours. If you'll have me.*

Would never have it any other way.

A man, Officer Stead based on his nametag, stepped from the group, weapon drawn.

The elder Popid, Fynn, spoke softly with no malice. "The Popids strive for peace. Please do not enter our village uninvited and set on causing harm."

Officer Stead didn't lower his weapon. "One of our frequent flyers has a house arrest ankle bracelet. She's allowed to travel between her apartment, her probation officer, and a job as long as it's within the government center. We lost her signal and had to track the backup beacon. Had the damnedest time finding her, finally had to call in assistance from the DPSFS to dig up your little hidden location."

"The Department is an ally, who would have led you to us?"

"We put out a call and got an answer and our helper offered their powers to get us into your little village. That's all you need to know."

"Which means you likely don't even know the

traitor who fed you the information. Seems a bad practice to trust intelligence from an untrustworthy source."

"They're trustworthy enough." Officer Stead shrugged.

"If they turned against the paranormal, supernatural, and fantasy community, then they are anything but trustworthy," Fynn stated.

"Our informant gave good intel as to the murders that happened in the far outer areas. Used their powers to round up the murderers and bring them in." The officer smirked. "Worked out well for the force. We got a bonus and didn't even have to go search the wastelands."

"The outer world hasn't said much about the murders since they happened," Fynn stated, clearly attempting to stall and distract. "Why wouldn't the capture of perpetrators be shared with the citizens?"

"Can't exactly tell the good folk we used corrupt members of the paranormal, supernatural, and fantasy worlds to land our perps." Stead shrugged.

"Can you even be assured that the individuals brought in were the ones behind the murders?" Fynn asked.

"Doesn't matter. We've got bodies in jail for the crime, and we got our bonus pay. End of story. Now, no more stalling." Officer Stead stepped forward, and the crew crowded menacingly behind him. Stead held up a hand. "We need your prisoner, and we'll be on our way.

If you don't comply in handing her over, we will be forced to search the village until we find what rightfully belongs to us."

"You have no jurisdiction in our village."

Officer Stead pulled a piece of paper from his back pocket. "We have a warrant."

"Your laws mean nothing to the Popids," Fynn said aloud, but I also heard them speak secretly to the village minds. *Prepare to defend the village. Attempt to defend and disarm. Our goal is nonviolence.*

"Once we find the girl, we'll be on our way." Officer Stead gestured with his arm. "Search the place."

The officers spread out and forced their way past the Popids closest to me.

"What do we do?" I whispered to Rhône.

"The Popids will use their powers to peacefully defend the village."

"I don't know how to do that."

"You may defend the village in whatever way seems best for you." Rhône and several others followed the officers and appeared to be casting blocking wards and protective charms to keep doors closed and drawers shut. Multiple chairs and tables were mysteriously moved to block and trip the officers. Many small items flew through the air, the officers batting at pens, trashcans, and notebooks swarming their heads.

I couldn't help but laugh at grown ass officers swatting at inanimate floating objects. When the officers used their weapons to swing at the objects or push at the tables blocking their way, suddenly their weapons were also floating or disappeared altogether. Popid magic seemed honed toward distraction and disarming. And watching uniformed, decorated men of the law hopping and jumping and grabbing at their floating weapons was quite entertaining. The sight before me seemed to lessen the hurt of their angry, hateful, bigoted words directed toward Rhône and the rest of the Popids. Words like *freaks, don't deserve to live,* and *unnatural* didn't come across quite as harmful as the speakers of said words were jumping like children for balloons just out of their reach.

But the Popids' magic wasn't enough to contain all of the crew. I noticed Stead circumventing his lackeys who were jumping like trained monkeys to travel down the hallway toward Dayne's holding cell. Was Stead aware of her location? Had the informant been able to give details about the village layout? My fists clenched as I broke from Rhône's side and followed Stead. Maybe the traitor in the village was the informant? I glanced back at the Popids disarming the police, and thought of the huge number of Popids working to strengthen the wards, cast new charms, and send positive energies to Mother Earth. Who among us would betray the village?

Rhône, stay here. I'm going to follow Stead. I sent my thoughts to Rhône as I trailed the officer.

"You had us worried, young lady," Officer Stead spoke to Dayne after busting the door open with the butt of his gun.

In an effort to keep the police from finding Dayne, the defending Popids had focused on the front area and left the back area completely opened; an easy target for Stead. An unwarded door and uncharmed lock stood no chance against the end of a long-gun.

"Get me out of here, please!" Dayne jumped to her feet. "I've got to get out and see my boss."

"We'll get you out of here, but you won't be going to a job any time soon." Stead reached for the keys to the cell on the wall.

"No! You don't understand. I work for a government official. I was here on official business," Dayne protested.

Dayne's boss being a government official wasn't surprising in the least, but the information didn't really narrow down anything for me.

"Well, official business or not, you broke the terms of your probation. Which means back to jail you go." The officer glanced around. "Actually, what you've got going for you here isn't half bad. Probably going to miss this place once you're locked up on the ground side. Government-run jailing isn't nearly as posh as this place." Stead jangled the keys and gripped the biggest of the four old-fashioned skeleton keys. "Let's see if this one works."

I couldn't just let him take Dayne. Could I? But if they got Dayne, they'd leave the village. We wanted them to leave the village.

Rhône, if we give them Dayne, they'll leave. We want them out of the village.

I sent my thoughts and hoped Rhône would hear me.

In the meantime, Stead was knocked off his feet when he attempted to put the key in the lock.

"Damn magic powers," he muttered. Reaching for his phone, he punched in a number and waited. A few seconds later, he barked, "We need you down here. There's a magic spell or some shit on this cell, and I can't get her out." He disconnected.

Kellan, if we simply hand Dayne over, we have no leverage to get them out of the village. We need to be in possession of what they want until we can lead them to the outer world and then do the exchange.

Rhône's words made sense.

There's a charm on the keys and lock. Stead can't get her out. How do I get to her and get her topside for the trade-off? Also, he's called for backup to help with the lock.

I rubbed the crystal charm in my pocket and thumbed the one on my neck.

"Officer, if you'll step aside, perhaps we can make a deal."

Stead and I both jerked our heads toward the voice.

Fynn stood calmly at the door.

"What kind of deal?" Stead narrowed his eyes at Fynn's words and shot a look of surprise toward me. He'd obviously been unaware of my presence.

"You take your men and go on up to the outer

world. We will bring the girl. When you're out of our village, you can have what you want. We have no need for her. We simply needed to hold her so as not to allow her to harm our people."

Stead laughed. "Okay, sure. We'll just go on up those stairs and wait for you to bring her to us. Do you think I'm stupid?"

Fynn's large eyes blinked slowly, and I fought the urge to giggle at how clearly I could read their emotions on that calm, quiet face.

"Young Kellan will transport the girl to the outer world along with one of your men. Your crew will follow. The exchange will take place outside of the village perimeter." Fynn nodded toward me as they spoke.

"Who is this guy? He doesn't look like the rest of you."

"I'm none of your business. If you want the girl, take the deal." I palmed the crystal in my pocket, ready to blast him if he came toward me or Fynn.

Stead made a quick call on his phone and barked, "Stand down." He then spoke into his radio, and we heard the "Stand down" squawk to the rest of his crew. "Fine. Let's get this show on the road."

"Kellan will pick the officer to help with the transport," Fynn stated with a force that allowed for no argument.

Stead looked as if he wanted to challenge, but grunted in agreement.

Fynn gestured for the officer to step aside. "Please step into the hallway. Dayne will be in Kellan's custody until we reach your men. Any attempt to remove her from his care will result in an automatic cancellation of this deal." Fynn waved a hand over the lock and the cell door swung open.

Dayne rushed toward me and threw herself into my arms. "Kellan!"

I removed her tentacles from around me, and grabbed a pair of handcuffs from behind the desk and tossed them to Fynn. "Cuff her, Fynn. She's not to be trusted."

"Kellan, no, you don't have to do that." Dayne wriggled in my grasp.

I ignored her words and assisted Fynn in cuffing her hands behind her back. I snaked my arm between her arms and her back and maneuvered her toward the door. "Stead, lead the way. I'll pick your man, and we'll get this over with."

Rhône, we're on our way to you.

When we reached the other officers, they stood anxiously awaiting Stead's orders, their weapons still floating out of reach.

"Give them their weapons back so we can leave," Stead demanded.

Rhône gestured to the other Popids to step back and every item above clattered to the ground. Rhône smirked and shrugged at the disgruntled men. "Sorry, your commander said to give them back. What goes up, must come down."

I sized up the officers and checked their nametags. "Butler, you're with me. We're taking the detainee to the outer world."

Butler, eyes wide, gaped at me and then sputtered. "Commander, can they do this?"

"Buck up, man. You're walking the girl up some stairs and through a waterfall. He didn't ask you to go to the outer regions with him," Stead grumbled.

Fynn spoke. "Kellan, upon reaching the village perimeter, let us know. We'll send the rest of the crew up to you."

I knew this little assignment was slightly more dangerous for me. Upon reaching the trade-off point, the officers could turn on me if they chose to. But if it meant keeping Rhône and the village safe, I was willing to risk it. And handing Dayne over to the authorities after what she'd done to Rhône was icing on the cake.

Butler, Dayne, and I reached the top of the cave steps just minutes later. The cool, damp air filled my lungs and soothed my nerves. The waterfall and cave were now my safe place.

I anticipated Butler's move long before he could even attempt it. Gripping the muscovite in my right hand, my left arm still restraining Dayne, I pulled the crystal from my pocket and pointed it toward Butler as he rushed me. The man jerked backwards so quickly, I feared I'd given him whiplash. "Get up. Try that again, and the deal is off," I commanded the man writhing on the wet cave floor.

Butler pulled himself to his feet and grumbled, "Damn it, I didn't think you were one of them. Fuckin' freaks."

"Kellan, what the hell was that?" Dayne demanded.

I ignored both of them and gestured Butler toward the waterfall. "Walk in front of me. We'll follow. Keep walking until you reach the grass at the far edge of the sidewalk."

Butler eyed me suspiciously, but with no other option, he walked forward and stepped around the very edge of the waterfall. I pushed Dayne through ahead of me. We reached the village perimeter, and I heard Rhône's words.

Kellan, can you see the falls? Leave Butler and Dayne and get back to the village. I'm sending the officers up, but don't let them see you. I think Stead has a plan to arrest you once he gets Dayne.

I wasn't surprised. I turned back toward the waterfall and saw it clear as day. The Popid magic was likely very weak.

"Beautiful, isn't it?" I threw my thumb over my shoulder at the falls.

Butler and Dayne looked at me in disgust. "What? The woods? Sure, Kel, it's great," Dayne snarled. "Can you get these cuffs off me?"

Maybe my powers were just stronger than I realized. I definitely saw the falls, but they clearly did not. I shrugged. "Nah, the police will take them off when they're good and ready." I turned and headed back toward the falls.

"Wait! Where are you going?" Dayne demanded.

"Back to the village." I waved over my shoulder.

"Where's the rest of my crew?" Butler hollered.

"On their way right now. Should be out in no time." I slipped behind the falls and clamored over the rocks to hide at the back of the cave just as Stead and the rest of his men were clomping up the stairs.

"Secure the girl. I'll apprehend the young man. I'm sure he's broken some sort of laws. We'll let the higher-ups determine his release." Stead waved an arm toward the waterfall. "Go on through, men. I'll follow."

I watched silently as the officers left the cave. *They're gone.*

Immediately, the cave filled with an energy I'd never felt before. The purple haze was dense, and the air was electric.

The wards are stronger than they've ever been. Come back to the village.

Rhône's words made me smile, and I all but skipped down the rock steps. The feeling of ensuing danger hadn't left the pit of my stomach, but Dayne was gone, and we'd protected the village from the police intrusion. I chose to focus on the positive.

THIRTEEN

WHEN I ROUNDED THE CORNER, planning to take Rhône to their room and sleep for several hours, I ran smack into Dr. Maeve Winston.

"Dr. Winston?" My brain stuttered as it tried to comprehend what Maeve was doing in the Popid village.

"Kellan, so good to see you." Maeve's eyes skittered to the two individuals who appeared to be accompanying her.

"What are you doing in the village?" This wasn't like running into someone at the store. You didn't just happen upon outsiders in the village. Even if the outsider was the head of the DPSFS.

"We came to offer our assistance," Maeve explained.

"How did you know there was a problem? Did a village elder call you?" Why would they call DPSFS? Popids were completely self-sufficient and needed very little from others. My brain continued to short-circuit like a motherboard doused in water.

Maeve pursed her lips. "Kellan, I'm the director of all things paranormal, supernatural, and fantasy. I know when the village is in trouble."

The two individuals behind her nodded sagely.

"Oh, um, okay." I mumbled, unsure of what to make of Maeve standing in the Popid village. "Well, um, we've got it all taken care of. The police have Dayne, and the village is safe. Probably best if you leave. The Popids will need their privacy to build up their magic again. Today took a lot out of us."

Maeve wrinkled her face. "We? Us? Kellan, what has gotten into you? This charade of you pretending to belong to the village has gone on long enough and has become quite embarrassing for all involved. I think it would be best if you came with me."

I jerked back as if she'd slapped me.

"Kellan will be going nowhere with you," Nayel thundered from nearby.

"Dr. Winston, you need to leave our village at once," Rube commanded.

Rhône stepped to my side and took my hand.

"Dr. Winston, I really appreciate all the help you gave me in the beginning. I was confused and had nowhere else to go. And thank you so much for getting me back to Rhône and the village. But you really don't belong here, and the Popids have asked you to leave." I lowered my voice and attempted to keep it respectful. "I really think you should go. The Popids have done nothing to you, please respect their home and their wishes."

"You ungrateful young man," Maeve exploded. "I've been beyond forthcoming with you in regards to the Popid village. I shared information that no mere human should have ever been given. Yet instead of using the knowledge I provided, you turned around and infiltrated a world in which you don't belong. You put me in a very difficult position. My momentary lack of judgment allowed for you to learn of a world you should have never known about. Yet now, I'm faced with removing you from the village and assigning consequences for your gross overstepping of boundaries in addition to completely taking advantage of my kindness."

Maeve's voice was loud and angry, and the village trembled from the negativity.

"Dr. Winston, please. You know that the village was just under attack. You know the Popids and their home thrives on the positivity of the earth. Your anger is putting chinks in an already weak armor. Please, just leave," I spoke lowly in an attempt to keep the peace.

"Kellan, the village will survive. Our fellow members are working tirelessly to build our energy. We will soon have a ceremony." Nayel placed a hand on my shoulder. "As unpleasant as this conversation has been, and will likely continue to be, Rube and I feel that it must be had."

I glanced between Nayel and Rube. Rhône squeezed my hand. *We are here for you. You one hundred percent belong in this place. Believe in yourself and trust your heart.*

I nodded to show I understood and yet my stomach continued to twist itself into knots.

"Dr. Winston, in all the years that the Popids have known you, you've always kept our treaties and agreements. Why now? Why betray us by leading the police to the village?" Rube crossed their arms over their chest.

Maeve scoffed. "I did no such thing," she stammered.

"And yet the very day our village is infiltrated by officers from the outer world, you show up," Nayel bit out.

"I stated clearly I came to offer my assistance and the support of the entire department. We *are* all on one team, you realize that, right?"

The village continued to tremble, lights dimmed in and out, and the feeling of unease in the pit of my stomach grew exponentially.

Is the village seriously okay? It seemed to get better for a moment, but now it's struggling. I brushed a thumb along Rhône's hand as I passed my thoughts their way.

The village is weak. I fear it will get weaker as truths and betrayals become clear. But the Popids and our fields are strong. We will overcome the struggle, embrace the positive light, and rise again. Rhône returned the caress with their answering thoughts.

A small group of Popids gathered near.

One spoke. "Elder Nayel, direct us as you see fit."

Nayel held up a hand. "Stand by. Prepare for a ceremony as you wait. Do not be alarmed. Our village may take a powerful hit, but we will scale the wall of negativity and weather any obstacle by the power of our Mother Earth."

"You have a traitor among you." Maeve snarled and pointed vaguely around the village. "They are the reason, the *culprit,* the one to blame for *all* of this."

"What nonsense do you speak?" Rube demanded.

"Have you not figured it out for yourselves?" Maeve sputtered. "One of your own is the reason for all of the pain, the hurt, the destruction."

I glanced at the Popids nearest me. Ximon blanched at Maeve's words. They were one of the most powerful Popids in the village, a sure bet for the next open seat with the elders. Definitely *able* to sabotage the village.

"Ximon." Disappointment laced my words. "But, why?"

Maeve laughed without humor at my words. "That one destroyed everything. Caused chaos and brought about so much sorrow and secrecy." Maeve's eyes welled with tears, but her jaw clenched and her face flushed in what was surely extreme anger. "Judas! Two-timer! Betrayer!"

Nayel and Rube turned toward Ximon.

"Ximon, is what she says true? Have you been

working against the village?" Rube's whispered words were raw with pain and outrage.

Nayel's nostrils flared. "Ximon, let down your blocks, let us hear you and know that she speaks only lies."

Ximon stood, unwavering, eyes bright and dark face stony.

Rube's breath shuddered, half sob, half growl.

"Take Ximon to the holding cell. Zie will need to be monitored at all times. Put our three strongest in the room. Ximon's powers are nearly endless." Nayel gave the command stoically, a solitary tear glittering on their cheek.

The village rumbled as if shaken by a violent earthquake. The suspicion of a traitor had been troublesome, but the uncovering of just who that traitor was had proven nearly devastating for the village both physically and emotionally.

"Dr. Winston, I will ask again for you to leave," Rube demanded.

I knew getting Maeve and her cohorts out of the village was of utmost importance so the Popids could focus all of their attention on strengthening the village and neutralizing Ximon.

"I'll leave," Maeve ground out, "but you need to know what you're dealing with. So many years, so many secrets, so many hurts and betrayals. You don't know what it will mean if the secrets come out. No one will be safe. We will all have to bow to the power. No one knows, no one but us, no one knows what we've gone through to keep it hidden, no one understands the pain, *my* pain..." Maeve was muttering incoherently by this point and her two companions, while appearing more like bodyguards, stepped into action and ushered Maeve up the stairs in caregiver fashion.

"What in the world," I murmured. "I feel like so much just happened, yet I'm more confused than ever."

Nayel took my free hand. "The village is so very weak. We must regroup, rejuvenate, and renew our energies. Rube and I have much to tell you, but after today, I feel we need more time to gather information before spilling incomplete counsel upon you." Nayel glanced at Rube, who nodded. "Kellan, with your permission, may we come together again in two days' time?"

"I need very much to know what is going on, but I trust you with my life. Complete and factual information is much appreciated, even if I have to wait for it. Two days, I can do that." I pulled Rhône close. "We can rest, heal, and help the village in the meantime."

———

"THE ROOM IS SECURE?" I shut the door to Rhône's private quarters.

"Yes, charmed and secure." Rhône assured with a slight smile.

I gathered Rhône in my arms and kissed them, rolling them under me on their bed. "I missed you, missed having you in my arms." I pushed up on my elbows. "Are you okay? Does this hurt?"

"I'm mostly healed, no, you're not hurting me." Rhône kissed my neck. "I missed touching you, having you near."

"I'm scared of what your parents have to tell me," I admitted.

"They have not brought me into their confidence as to the information they hold. However, I do not sense any of it is devastating or destructive. Perhaps startling and maybe it will change some things, but I don't believe the news is terrible."

I kissed Rhône's cheek. "I'll do my best to take comfort in that for now."

"You could take comfort in me," Rhône suggested with a sly smile.

"You've been injured. I told your parents we were resting."

"I've been healing. We'll rest after. And we can go slow and easy." Rhône kissed me. "Please, Kellan, my body craves the connection." Zie spread their legs, making room for me, and our cocks bumped together.

Immediately, my dick came to instant attention and my blood began to sizzle. "Let me make sure I've got this right," I teased, whispering against Rhône's ear, thrusting my cock against theirs. "You'd like me to take my rock-hard, throbbing cock and slide it ever so slowly deep into your ass, pumping in and out of your sweet hole in purposefully slow motion, stroking your dick with my fist, until your body can take no more and you fall apart, coming all over my hand as my cock explodes and spills into your ass."

Rhône moaned, thrusting their hips up to meet my cock. "Kellan," they groaned.

"Did I get it right? Is that what you're wanting?"

"Yes, please. Please, Kellan, please. Now." Rhône writhed under me.

Stripping their clothes, slowly, I placed kisses along zir slightly shimmery skin. When Rhône was completely naked, I stood and undressed as slowly as possible, enjoying the scene on the bed. Rhône bit zir lip and stroked their cock, legs open and waiting for me to fill them.

Crawling back onto the bed, I took my place between their legs. "I'm going to fuck you so gentle and slow, you're going to beg me to let you come."

Rhône whimpered.

I positioned their arms above their head and caught their wrists in one of my hands. "No touching." My cockhead nudged Rhône's hole, and I pressed gently until their body opened and allowed my thick, throbbing invasion.

Driving Rhône insane with slow, gentle lovemaking was amazing. Driving *myself* insane with the same thing was almost too much. I thrust in and out in agonizingly slow motion, capturing Rhône's moans with my kisses, their legs wrapped around me, and their cock leaking between us.

"Kellan, please, stroke me. Let me come," Rhône begged.

Knowing I had very few thrusts left before I lost it, I took Rhône in my fist and began to pump in the same slow rhythm. "Come for me, baby. Let go."

Rhône shuddered, head thrown back, and spilled hot seed over my fingers and their stomach. With a final thrust into their waiting body, I stilled and erupted my own release in thick, hot spurts.

I collapsed onto Rhône, our sweaty, sticky bodies breathing heavily.

"So, that was amazing, right?" I whispered.

"The most amazing," Rhône agreed.

"I'm thinking it's a positive when we do that, in any form, yeah?"

Rhône chuckled. "I'm feeling pretty euphoric and positive, yes. Why?"

I shrugged. "Just thinking we could assist in building the village's strength back up. Do our part, you know? Sex as an offering to Mother Earth?"

Rhône laughed. "It actually works. Maybe not enough to completely heal the village, but every little bit helps."

"Maybe we should have a whole Mother Earth Orgy Offering."

Rhône laughed harder. "Let's not get carried away.

I'm not willing to share you in an orgy, so Mother Earth can just get good vibes another way."

"Blasphemous!" I teased and gently pulled out of Rhône's body. "Let's clean up. Then I feel a nap of at least two days is in store."

"And food?" Rhône suggested.

My stomach growled. "Food. Yes, let's do food first, then nap. I figure I better build up my emotional strength before Nayel and Rube sit me down and change my life forever."

FOURTEEN

FOR TWO DAYS, the village struggle to rejuvenate. We wandered the village and saw small groups of Popids doing their part to strengthen their home. Many focused their efforts to increase and tighten charms and wards, some worked on creating new magic, some gathered together for small ceremonies to send positivity to Mother Earth, and many labored tirelessly in the popid fields in hopes of keeping the crop strong.

"Has it ever been this bad?" I whispered to Rhône.

"In some ways, yes." Rhône nodded. "But I'm not sure we've ever had so many negative complications piled on at once. This betrayal feels as if it's the hardest to overcome, the hardest to understand." The Popids were physically and emotionally spent; the village suffered the same.

"Do you think Ximon will ever explain? Have a good

reason?" I stared out at the glorious purple popid fields stretching for as far as the eye could see.

Rhône pressed their lips together and shrugged. "I'm unsure. So far, Ximon isn't talking."

Nayel hurried up behind us. "I apologize for both interrupting *and* eavesdropping, but Kellan, I must ask you for a favor."

I nodded. "Of course."

"Ximon has requested to speak to you."

My eyes nearly popped from their sockets. "What? Why?"

Nayel shook their head. "I don't know. But the team questioning Ximon just informed me of the request."

"Of course, I'll help," I quickly agreed, but I was confused and anxious.

"I don't feel that Kellan should be with Ximon alone," Rhône stated. "Ximon's powers are stronger than mine, stronger than even some of the elders. I worry for Kellan's safety."

"Agreed," Nayel replied. "The team has been working to neutralize Ximon's powers, but Kellan should not be alone with zir." Nayel turned to me. "Ximon is one of our most powerful; they've hidden their thoughts with strong charms and spells so we have no way of knowing their intent in speaking to you."

It was decided I would sit outside of Ximon's holding cell while the Popid team gathered around to weaken Ximon's powers and protect me.

I approached Ximon's cell with care. Their light hair was much shorter than Rhône's, but they had a very long, almost white, beard that reached to mid stomach. Ximon's skin was much darker than Rhône's but had the same shimmery purple as the rest of the village, and their dark eyes flashed as I came near.

"Hello," I said softly and raised a hand in greeting. "You wanted to see me?"

Ximon stared at me for what seemed like forever. When I began to squirm and glanced at the rest of the Popids for reassurance, Ximon finally spoke.

"You are the one. I've watched you in the village."

I raised my brows. "The one what?"

Ximon waved off my question.

"They don't know." Ximon chuckled. "Or maybe they do. They definitely didn't learn from me. I've kept my mind vaulted; no secrets can escape."

"Who doesn't know, and what do they not know?" I was frustrated. Ximon seemed to be speaking in riddles.

"They'll find out. Then they will be sorry. I had my reasons for keeping quiet. Secrets and hidden truths are sometimes better left that way. The powers will soon be recognized, and then everyone will wish the secret had stayed hidden." Ximon studied me and reached a hand through the bars.

I glanced at Nayel before I stood and extended my hand. Ximon gripped my hand in theirs. Without warning, I dropped to my knees, my vision filled with flashes of light interspersed between images. Visions of the waterfall, the cave, Popids, and the elder council were followed by darker, fuzzier images of government buildings, extra-sapien beings, and me in the middle of a Popid ceremony with Rhône by my side. Touching Ximon didn't hurt, but the images zinged through my mind like an electric current before Nayel reached for me and jerked me from Ximon's grasp.

"What was that, Ximon?" Nayel demanded.

I stood on shaky knees and backed away from the cell.

"I request to be returned to the fields," Ximon stated, ignoring Nayel's question.

The Popids around me gasped.

"No, Ximon," Fynn pleaded. "You are our family. You have made grievous mistakes, but the village must first accept your atonement before you may make amends."

"A Popid can request, at any time, to be returned to the fields. I am of sound mind and body, and my desire is for exactly that."

"Ximon, there is no return from what you're asking," Nayel spoke softly. "Surely what you have done is not so abhorrent that you can't recover."

"That which I have done is what I felt was best for both myself, the village, and all involved. I have no desire to participate in a trial having all of my deepest secrets revealed. My time with the Popids is drawing near. I ask for my wishes to be respected."

Fynn spoke again. "You know that we will eventually learn of all you are hiding."

"Yes," Ximon replied. "And I wish to not be here. While I stand by what I did, I do not wish to experience the sadness and disappointment my actions will bring." Ximon glanced at me. "There will be confusion, worry, and fear. I wish not to take part."

"You're a coward," I accused. "I don't know what you did specifically, but I know you went against your people. A traitor. And now you don't have the backbone to stand trial for what you did."

Ximon shrugged.

"What happened to you?" I continued. "The Popids are loving, kind, caring, and open. What made you so aloof, so cool, so indifferent?"

"Generations of watching humanity destroy itself and Earth. Watching the in-fighting among extra-sapiens. Humans have done nothing but take, and take, and take. They hate, they ruin, they destroy. And are we extra-sapiens much better?"

Nayel interrupted. "Surely you can see the good in our world, the extra-sapien worlds, and even the human world? It's not *all* bad."

Ximon shook their head. "For every good I see, there are a thousand bad. For every positive step forward, there are two, three, four steps back. Even in our perfect village, we must work so very hard for simple survival all because of the negativity of this planet. It's too much."

"But love, friendship, fellowship? What of those?" Nayel persisted.

Ximon smiled slightly. "I loved once. But a beautiful thing turned ugly and hateful, and I couldn't risk destroying that which I held most dear." Zir shook their head. "Now, my stories are over. Please respect my request and return me to the popids."

Fynn spoke up. "You will recall from your elder training that a request like yours isn't taken lightly and does not get carried out quickly. There is a waiting period. Until then, you will stay here as you are, unfortunately, a flight risk. When the requirements are met, your request will be fulfilled."

We left Ximon and a small group of Popids who would continue to question and also disarm Ximon's magic the best they could.

"He was making no sense." I ran my hand over my face. "I mean, I can understand all that Ximon said about the world's negativity. But the stuff being spewed before that made no sense at all. I heard their words, but it was like they were talking gibberish."

Rhône squeezed my hand. "I believe that, in due time, all will be revealed."

"What does *return to the popids* mean?"

Rhône looked at me, eyes solemn.

I ran the statement through my head again and again. And then it hit me.

"Oh," I breathed with wide eyes. "Oh." My heart hurt, but I was also angry. "Ximon admits they weren't loyal, but now they just get to...to...basically off themselves in order to escape condemnation and consequences?"

"Returning to the fields isn't necessarily easier or better," Rhône assured. "In fact, while we Popids don't *know* what happens when a soul returns to the flowers, it is thought that an individual *choosing* to return to the popids, especially in a case of wrongdoing like this, it is believed that being will perhaps suffer for eternity, or at least exist in limbo until their next calling."

"Their next calling?"

"It is our belief that many Popids who perish will one day be called to return. Perhaps as a villager, perhaps as something else." Rhône shrugged. "Ximon will not be getting off easy by returning to the popids if our beliefs are correct."

I thought over their words. "So, Ximon could get a second chance?"

"It is possible. But, in Ximon's case, it would be a second chance given only in order to right the wrongs." Rhône directed me toward a room I'd never been in.

A long table sat at the front of the room. Decorated with a purple velvet cloth, the table was flanked by ten solid oak chairs and held vases of popids along with pitchers of what appeared to be water and popid tea.

"What is this place?" I whispered. I wasn't sure why, but it seemed important to be respectful and quiet.

"This is Elder Hall. This is where trials take place. It's also where the most important meetings occur,"

Rhône explained just as the door opened and the elders filed in.

"Why are we here?"

Rhône squeezed my hand again. "My parents and the elders have information for you."

My eyes widened. "Oh," I whispered. I took a deep breath. "I'm not sure I'm ready for this."

"You are. You are strong and powerful, and I am by your side, always."

I swallowed and nodded. "Okay, then. Let's do this."

FIFTEEN

ONCE THE ELDERS had been seated, Rhône and I took our place before them.

Nayel spoke first, "The elder council has been hard at work gathering information, not just for young Kellan, but also for the good of the village. We have been able to answer some of our questions, but many of the answers have given way to new questions that must be studied."

Rube stood. "I'd prefer this meeting to be less formal. Can we all move into a circle formation?"

The elders moved from their table, and we all gathered our chairs into a circle. Water and popid tea were passed around.

Rube smiled. "That's better. Let us begin."

"Our top seers and empaths were tasked with determining how Dayne and the police were able to breach the village," Fynn began. "Dayne was wearing an ankle bracelet from a recent arrest. She was able to get into the village due to having a vague knowledge of its location."

I sighed. "I'm sorry, that's my fault."

"No, not completely." Fynn shook their head. "Dayne's boss—we'll get to that more later—had also shared the general vicinity of the falls. When Dayne took out Rhône, the village's strength weakened and allowed for the breach."

"So how did the police infiltrate the cave?" Rhône asked.

"The police were able to track Dayne's location because of the ankle bracelet. When they realized Dayne was somewhere in the vicinity, they contacted the DPSFS and asked for assistance." Fynn paused. "While we do not have one hundred percent conclusive evidence at this point, it does appear that Dr. Maeve Winston used her powers within the department, along with her personal powers, to breach the village and allow the police inside."

My stomach sank. "Dr. Winston is supposed to be on the good side," I mumbled. "How could she put the village at risk?"

"We hope to get further information from Maeve soon," Nayel interjected. "Unfortunately, it appears Dr. Winston is one of many lessons in understanding things are not always as they seem."

I nodded, feeling sad and confused.

The door opened and a Popid entered. "The transmission is ready."

Nayel nodded. "Good." They pointed to the middle of the circle. "We are not comfortable inviting Dr. Winston back into Popid territory, but we've asked her to speak to us through the use of combined powers."

A holographic-type image of Maeve appeared inside the circle.

"This is unheard of and a sign of disrespect toward the highest office of our people," Maeve bit out.

"Thank you for coming, Dr. Winston," Rube began, ignoring Maeve's outrage. "We have questions for you. We'd like for these questions to be answered truthfully and completely so as not to have to involve the DPSFS board of directors. I feel your colleagues would be quite disappointed if they were to be involved in this investigation due to your poor judgement."

"Investigation?" Maeve all but shrieked.

"Unofficial for now," Nayel assured. "But questions remain, and you are our best source for the answers."

Maeve's nostrils flared. "Let's get on with it then."

"How long have you known Kellan carried extra-sapien blood?" Fynn asked softly, but regardless of the tone, the question wasn't optional; it was a demand.

I gasped. "What?"

Rhône took my hand and squeezed. *Shhh, let her talk. There is much for you and us to learn.*

Maeve's gaze darted to mine. "Since he was born."

My heart nearly pounded out of my chest. "Oh my God," I whispered.

"Who has been responsible for keeping Kellan out of the DPSFS?" Fynn's raised voice boomed across the room.

"I have." Maeve's body vibrated with anger. "You don't understand. There were reasons I did what I did."

Nayel scanned the room, gauging the mood of the crowd. "We'd like to hear your reasons."

Maeve glanced around, eyes wide, as if determining her next move. "I'm not prepared to discuss this right now." She held up her hand to silence the protests. "Many things are going to change after I tell my story. While I had hoped it wouldn't come to this, I feared it one day would. Please allow me a day to put my affairs in order. I will return. You should also call on Maris Winston of the outer world government. She should be involved in your questioning."

The holograph disappeared, and we were left in silence.

"Maris Winston? Maeve's sister?" I questioned. "But how is Maris part of *my* government if Maeve is the head of all things extra-sapien?" My head spun.

"We will meet again in one day." Nayel placed a reassuring hand on my shoulder. "We'll call on Maris Winston. I have a strong hope that all questions will soon be answered."

The elders were dismissed, leaving just Nayel, Rube, Rhône, and me.

"Kellan, something is likely to come out when Maeve returns. The knowledge is going to be surprising and possibly hurtful, but we'd like permission to share with you *now* rather than have you find out in front of everyone," Rube spoke softly.

My stomach churned. "Oh God," I breathed out. "I don't know if I want to know."

Rhône wrapped their arms around my waist and pressed against my side. "We are here to support you. Perhaps learning the information now and having time to process it will be better in the long run?"

I took a deep breath and nodded. "Yeah, you're probably right." I hugged Rhône close with one arm and rubbed the crystal in my pocket with my other hand. "Go ahead. I want to know."

Nayel smiled softly. "In all of our research and digging, we found that your parents are not your birth parents."

The words shocked me, yet somehow, this was the first thing to make sense in a very long time. The knowledge explained my burgeoning powers and the existence of extra-sapien blood in my veins. I nodded. "Okay, that almost comes as a relief. Some sort of explanation for my lifelong draw to all things extra-sapien. Do you know who my biological parents are?"

"We are not completely certain. Those are questions we will save for Maeve. We believe she knows much about your parentage and, as a result, she's been the one keeping you out of the DPSFS for so many years." Rube patted my shoulder.

"But it would correlate that at least one or both of my biological parents are extra-sapien." A vein in my neck throbbed and I hoped no one would see how much I feared the truth.

"Yes, at this point, we feel that both parents are likely from an extra-sapien bloodline. We have our suspicions, but feel it best to wait to hear from Maeve."

"Maeve said she's known about me my entire life. And that she's been the one keeping me out of the DPSFS." I ran a hand over my face. "Why? Why would she do that?" All this time. I had wanted nothing more than to belong, find my place. And Maeve Winston, someone I thought I could trust, had kept me from what I wanted the most.

"We don't know for sure," Nayel stated. "We will be finding out the details to this turn of events for the first time right alongside you."

"Do my parents, my real parents, not my bio parents, do they know I'm extra-sapien?" Oh God, if I found out they'd kept me from my bloodline, my calling, I didn't know what I'd do.

Rube shook their head. "No, dear. From what we've been able to gather, your adopted parents..."

"My *real* parents," I interjected.

"Your *real* parents," Rube continued, "adopted you from a government run agency as a newborn. They knew nothing about your bloodline. They simply longed for a child and were overjoyed to be blessed with you."

"I should talk to them— go see them," My heart beat so fast I couldn't catch my breath.

Rube offered me a wane smile. "I would suggest you wait until you know more details, but if you feel the need to see them, of course you should go."

I thought it over for a moment. "No, you're right. It would be best to go to them with all my questions answered. Bombarding them with enquiries they likely can't answer would do me no good."

We stood silently for several heartbeats.

I inhaled deeply, calming my panic. "This is all very overwhelming and surreal."

Rhône started to speak, but their voice broke. They cleared their throat and began again. "Let's retire to my room. We can rest and rejuvenate, prepare ourselves for Maeve and Maris and whatever information they may bring us."

"That sounds like a good idea," I replied, suddenly very sleepy. "I'm not sure my brain or heart can take any more for today."

The four of us left Elder Hall and retired to our rooms.

After a slow, sensual, relaxing shower, Rhône and I cuddled into bed. I wanted to talk, wanted to kiss and hold Rhône, but I fell asleep within seconds of my head hitting the pillow.

———

I WOKE SLOWLY. I wanted to wake every damn day with Rhône in my arms. I rocked my hard length into Rhône's. "Good morning," I whispered.

They smiled and thrust into me. "Morning."

I slipped my hands under Rhône's sleep shorts and gripped their ass cheeks before sliding the shorts down. Rhône's hands squirmed under my waistband and lowered my pants. Our hot, naked cocks rubbed together. My hand gripped our dicks and pumped, Rhône's smaller hand covering mine.

We thrust and moaned, pumped and panted. The stress and uncertainty of the last several days and weeks were forgotten as I found pleasure in Rhône. I let our love overcome the unknown and let what I'd found with them assure me that everything would be okay.

I trailed my hand from our cocks to Rhône's wet core. Sliding in two fingers, I stroked and teased until my fingers were slick with their wetness. Dragging the moisture along zir skin, I rubbed gently at Rhône's hole before pressing softly until they opened for me.

"Stroke me. Jack us off," I whispered. "Come for me, Rhône."

As Rhône continued to pump our hard lengths in their fist, I pressed two wet fingers slowly in and out of their ass. My balls drew up tight, and I prepared for release.

"I'm going to blow, Rhône," I warned. "Come with

me." I continued thrusting until my release washed over me in waves, spurting between our bodies, Rhône's ass clenching against my fingers.

When I had recovered and caught my breath, I murmured, "I love you. No matter what I learn about my parents, I love you and can take on anything with you by my side."

"Good, because by your side is where I plan to spend the rest of my life." Rhône kissed me softly. "And I have a good feeling about what you're going to learn. It may be a lot to take in all at once, but I think the end result is going to be amazing."

We showered and went to the kitchen to gather breakfast. We spent much of the rest of the day in bed, relaxing and preparing our minds for what we were about to learn.

————

MAEVE'S HOLOGRAM appeared in the meeting room first, followed soon by another image. An exact image. Maris Winston was Maeve's *identical twin* sister.

My brain tried to make sense of the bombardment of information.

"Sister," Maeve stated and gave Maris a terse nod. Maeve was perhaps slightly plumper than Maris. Her sister had darker hair and a somewhat more refined look than Maeve. But there was no question they were twins.

Had I seen Maris alone, I would have thought she was Maeve.

Maris returned the curt nod—clearly there was no love lost between the two—before addressing the council. "I want the record to reflect that I am here of my own accord. I had the right to demand legal representation, but I declined. Things I will tell you today will paint myself and my sister in a very bad light. This is something I have forever hoped to avoid, but it appears poor choices and bad decisions on my part have finally caught up to me. I request that you keep in mind my willingness to cooperate and provide information in hopes that you don't take legal action against me."

"I request the same," Maeve chimed in.

"The Popids reserve the right to enact legal action, but your cooperation will be taken into account," Nayel stated. "Shall we begin?"

Maeve and Maris nodded in unison.

"For the record, Maeve Winston and Maris Winston have appeared of their own accord to answer questions pertaining to the parentage of Kellan Roberts, the sabotage of Kellan's continued application to the Department of Fantasy, Supernatural, and Paranormal Sciences, and their knowledge of and/or involvement with the traitorous Popid, Ximon," Fynn spoke officially and clearly.

"Dr. Maeve Winston, you previously stated you had known of Kellan's extra-sapien blood since his birth. Is this still your stance?" Nayel asked.

Maeve nodded. "Yes. I knew of Kellan's parentage even before he was born."

My eyes widened, and I glanced around the room. Wide eyes and slightly opened mouths were all I saw.

Maris' gaze landed on me for a brief second before she turned away.

"Please start at the beginning of your knowledge of Kellan," Rube interjected.

Rhône had been holding my hand but now squeezed it tightly.

Maeve settled her features into a mask of calm and looked directly at me. "Kellan, please know that nothing I did was ever meant to hurt you. My actions were the result of hatred, a broken heart, and the desire to preserve my position within the extra-sapien community." She held a hand to her cheek. "When I met you, saw what a fine young man you were, read your emotions and how good, open, kind, and accepting you were, I began to doubt the years I spent keeping you out of the department, out of our world."

I could only nod and swallow thickly.

Rube shifted in their chair and waved a hand toward Maeve. "Please continue."

Maeve took a deep breath. "I was very much in love a long time ago. This person and I made promises to each other, we had plans, we would join our powers and rise to the very top." She paused and threw a hateful look toward Maris. "My sister, who was supposed to be the one person in my life I could trust and count on, had denied her powers and signed away her position within the DPSFS and taken a very lofty position within the human government. Little did I know that my dear sister had also been seeing the love of my life behind my back."

Maris folded her arms across her chest. "Maeve, stop with the sappy soap opera. It happened a long time ago."

"You stole the only being to ever love me for me!" Maeve shrieked, her finger pointing at Maris. "Why? Just to prove you could? Surely not because you felt love. You've never shown an ounce of love for anything in this life aside from yourself."

Maris rolled her eyes. "It started as a simple case of mistaken identity. Your *true love* thought I was you. I enjoyed the attention to begin with and thought it could be a fun little distraction from the weight of my job. I didn't realize it would turn into something so serious."

"Did you also not realize that you could get pregnant? How stupid could you be?" Maeve gestured wildly.

The Popids and I sat, transfixed, as the sisters' story played out before us as if we were the audience of a stage play.

"Pregnancy was *not* in the plan. It was simply supposed to be fun while it lasted," Maris whispered.

"Fun? Fun at my expense! Fun that led to my broken heart!" Maeve shouted.

"Must we really rehash this every damn time we're together?" Maris' voice would have dried Lake Huron.

"Ladies, while I can understand this is quite an emotional and tense topic, let's try to stay focused on Kellan's part in all of this," Fynn interrupted quietly.

I took a deep breath and licked my lips, my heart rattling in my ribcage.

"Maris got pregnant. My former lover was the father of her baby. I knew from the moment Maris admitted sleeping with my lover and became pregnant that I had to hide the baby's parentage. The baby would be stronger and more powerful than any lifeform. I decided from the very beginning that I would do everything within my power to keep the child from the department. If he wasn't allowed in the department, he'd never discover or hone his powers, and my position would be safe; I knew his powers would exceed mine ten-fold." Maeve hung her head. "I also never wanted anyone to know I had been betrayed by my own sister, that my lover had chosen *her* over me, and they now shared a child." Maeve's voice broke as she gestured weakly toward Maris.

Maris sighed and looked to the floor. "We never planned any of what happened to turn out the way it did."

I stood up. "So, I was just an unfortunate consequence of your poor decisions?" My words quivered, but Rhône stood and took my hand, giving me strength. "You threw me away? Why? Because you didn't want me? Couldn't be reminded of your little tryst on the wild side? Couldn't be tied down with baggage that would keep you from climbing the government ladder?" My voice rose with each question. "Had to get rid of your dirty little secret, huh? Because we all know no extra-sapien can be part of the human government system. And a government employee fuckin' around with an extra-sapien being is a huge no-no. Better to just get rid of me, cover the evidence, hope that I never felt my powers or learned to use them?" I took a step toward the holograph. "The *only* good thing you've ever done is give me up for adoption so that I could find love and acceptance with my *real* parents."

Maris stared, the look in her eyes ice-cold.

Maeve's shoulders shook and she turned away, her sobs echoing.

"And you. Look at me Maeve." My rage threatened, and I had to collect myself. "You! Keeping me from my bloodline, keeping my parentage secret, hiding my powers all these years? All because you were afraid I'd become more powerful than you? All so you could save face? You're just as bad as your sister."

"I know, I know," Maeve sniffed and fished in her pocket for a tissue. "It was selfish, and I feared this day would come. I'm sorry for the pain I've caused you. I had hoped that sharing the Popids with you would bring you happiness, maybe be a consolation for all I had kept you from. I didn't plan on you becoming so entrenched with their people. Didn't plan for them to take such a liking to an outsider." Maeve sighed. "But I should have known. Should have known they'd welcome you with open arms. Should have known your heart would find a home with them." She shook her head as if mocking her own ignorance. "Should have known they'd sense your powers."

"Maeve, you hid Kellan's bloodline and sabotaged his applications to your department out of fear he'd one day become more powerful than you. And also, to cover up the fact that your sister and lover had betrayed you. Is that correct?" Fynn restated what we'd heard from Maeve.

"Yes," Maeve agreed.

"And, Maris, you allowed Maeve to do these things knowing that if Kellan's parentage was ever discovered, you would lose your place in the government both because you were involved with an extra-sapien *and* because you carry extra-sapien blood yourself. Is that correct?" Fynn asked.

"Yes." Maris sighed. "Kellan, I do apologize. You were never a living, breathing being to me. I refused to accept your existence throughout the entire pregnancy, refused to even look at you when you were born. Never accepting you as a real person made it easier to give you up, to turn a blind eye. As long as you never found out who you really were, my life as I knew it would continue and all would be well." Maris pressed her lips together. "I kept tabs on you, but only to be sure you never had the chance to discover your true bloodline.

But seeing you here today, standing before me in the flesh, I realize what a poor decision I made all those years ago. My bad choices should not have determined your course in life."

My nostrils flared, and I clenched my jaw so tightly I feared it would pop. I took a deep breath. "I'm beyond angry at what the two of you did. You've kept me from my rightful place in the extra-sapien community." I ran a hand over my hair. "But I choose to believe and think positively that the events in my life leading up to this point have all been for the best. I have the most amazing parents a guy could ask for, *and* I've found the love of my life who I will *never* be without." I gripped Rhône's hand tightly. "So, while I'll never forget what you've done, I can most definitely forgive." I smiled. "You may ask yourself how or why. I can forgive because I choose to be positive, I choose to be happy, and I choose to send only good to our Mother Earth. Without your terrible decisions, I wouldn't have Rhône and the Popids in my life, and I can never regret any of that."

"I feel that one question still remains before we allow Kellan some time to process," Nayel spoke up.

I glanced between Maris, Maeve, Nayel, Rube, and Rhône. "Who is my father?"

But as the words left my mouth, my brain processed the answer my heart already knew.

"Ximon, Ximon is my father," I whispered.

"Yes," Maeve bit out. "We were in love, going to rule

the extra-sapien world. Until Ximon and my sister betrayed me. As penance for cheating on me and being irresponsible enough to get Maris pregnant, Ximon devoted zir life to keeping Kellan's parentage a secret." She chuckled. "I got a good laugh when Kellan discovered the village, and Ximon came to me distressed over the charms, wards, and spells they were having to block or create just to keep Kellan and the Popids from figuring it all out. While I didn't want Kellan to come to power and take my place, I found great joy in making Ximon suffer."

"I have a Popid as a parent, an extra-sapien mother who rejected her powers in order to be part of the most corrupt government this world has ever known, and an aunt who holds the highest, most powerful position in the DPSFS." I ticked the facts on my fingers and took a deep breath.

"Don't forget you're also likely soon to be the most powerful Popid and take your place as head of the DPSFS as well," Rhône chimed in with a smile while Maeve and Maris gritted their teeth.

I nodded slowly. "So, I'm going to need *a lot* of processing time. Is this meeting over?"

Rhône smiled and hugged me to their side.

"The Popid council will send their findings to the extra-sapien governing body leaders, the DPSFS board, and the outer world government." Fynn rose. When Maeve and Maris both protested, Fynn held up a hand. "We will note that you spoke to us of your own accord and were forthcoming with the details we needed. Beyond that, the consequences handed down will be up to each organization with which you've broken policy."

"I think you can agree that is beyond fair," Nayel interjected.

Maeve and Maris both mumbled their agreements, and their holographs disappeared.

"Are you okay?" Rube asked, a hand on my shoulder.

I took a deep breath and ran everything through my head. I nodded slowly. "Yeah. It's a lot to take in. And I'm sure it will take a while to grasp everything. But overall, I'm feeling okay."

A line of elders filed past me, each laying a hand on my shoulders until Rhône and I were alone with Rube and Nayel.

"Is it bad that I'm slightly relieved? And maybe somewhat excited?" My tone was subdued, trying to make sense of how I was feeling. "It's as if a lifelong dream is finally coming true."

"There are no right or wrong feelings here, Kellan." Nayel patted my arm. "Your reaction and feelings are *yours*, and we respect them."

"I can definitely understand feeling relief and excitement," Rhône added. "I feel the same excitement in knowing we've only seen the beginning of your powers. *You*, Kellan Roberts, are destined for great things, and I feel honored to know I'll be by your side as you reach each milestone."

"And I never want you anywhere but by my side as I

begin this long-awaited journey." I leaned down and kissed Rhône before turning to hug Nayel and Rube.

"I think we could all use some time to rest," Rube suggested. "We will prepare for a ceremony tomorrow night. We have much good to send to Mother Earth."

SIXTEEN

THE CEREMONY WAS EXACTLY what I needed to regroup and recharge my positivity. The village nearly trembled with goodness, and my heart, in turn, swelled to the point where I had no room for the negative thoughts taking root after learning who my parents were.

"You know, it's not so much that I'm upset Maris and Ximon are my parents. I'm not even upset they didn't raise me. I ended up with the parents I was supposed to be with." I reached for Rhône's hand. "I'm angry and sad at all the time they took from me. The years where I felt alone, struggling, wanting so badly to belong to the extra-sapien world. I could have been learning and perfecting my powers all that time."

Rhône nodded at my words as we drank cold, refreshing popid tea and watched the dancing we'd recently stepped away from. "I can understand your anger and your frustration."

I glanced at Rhône. "But?"

They smiled softly. "How do you know there's a but?"

I leaned in and nuzzled zir cheek. "Haven't you noticed we're getting pretty good at communicating with no words. Sometimes I feel like we speak best when we say nothing at all, if that even makes sense."

"It does, and yes, we are getting pretty good at silent communication. Spoken words aren't always needed when you have a connection like ours." Rhône pressed their cheek into my lips.

"So, the but?"

Rhône smirked. "While I agree you *did* miss out on a lot of years of learning and perfecting your powers, I also think the way you grew up, functioning as a mere human..."

My snort interrupted Rhône's train of thought. "Sorry," I mumbled with a grin. "It's just weird to think I'm not just a human. I actually have extra-sapien blood."

"Not just extra-sapien blood. You have the blood of one of the most powerful Popids ever known *and* the sister of Dr. Maeve Winston. Even though Maris never claimed her powers, they were, and always will be, in her blood. If Maeve Winston is powerful enough to be the head of all things fantasy, supernatural, and paranormal, Maris likely has similar powers. Which means your extra-sapien blood is likely *extra* extra-sapien." Rhône winked. "And like I was saying before I was interrupted," they teased, "I think your background and history as a human plus extra-sapien blood and powers will be instrumental in your future success as a leader of the fantasy, supernatural, and paranormal community."

I stared at Rhône for what seemed like an eternity, waiting on them to crack a smile, let me know they were joking. Zie did none of those things. "You're hilarious," I scoffed with a roll of my eyes.

Rhône frowned. "What? I'm not trying to be funny."

"Leader of even the DPSFS is an extreme longshot, but being a successful leader of the fantasy, supernatural, and paranormal community? That's absolutely absurd." I shook my head and drained the glass of tea.

Rhône touched my shoulder and dipped their face to make eye contact with me. "You're kidding, right?"

I raised my brows in question.

"Kellan, do you seriously not understand what your parentage will afford you? Where your bloodline will take you?"

I shrugged. "I assumed it would mean I get to at least be somewhat a part of the Popid village. Maybe finally get a job at the DPSFS. What else?"

Rhône smiled softly. "You are absolutely adorable. And your cluelessness is another one of your strengths."

"I'm strong because I'm clueless?" I laughed.

"Maybe clueless isn't the right word. It's your lack of pretentiousness. You expect nothing from your bloodline, your powers, you don't even assume this new information is going to change your life in so many amazing ways."

"Why would I assume or expect the other leaders of the department or the extra-sapien community would look to me for *anything*? I've been nothing but a human, a simple custodian, just trying to survive for my whole life. I have nothing. I am nothing special. Okay, so I have extra-sapien blood, but I don't see how that's going to launch my career or lock in my future success."

Rhône shook their head. "Well, just as we've always told you not to question your specialness, I'll tell you right now that you may as well prepare for and get used to the fact that you will soon be a top-level leader within the Popid village, the extra-sapien community, *and* the DPSFS. Period."

"Rhône, I love you very much, and I value your opinion. I also adore how much you believe in me, but I'm pretty sure you've got a bad case of bias going on here." I kissed the side of their face. "Let's just enjoy the fact that my dream of being part of your world has finally come true and maybe plan on how I'll learn all there is to know."

"You silly, silly man." Rhône quirked their lips and shook their head. "I speak not from my love for you or my extreme bias of how amazing you are, but from the position of one of the top Popids. You were born to be a leader. So, you came to it somewhat late. That doesn't mean you're not our next great leader."

"Anyone who would promote me to anything more than maybe a project manager is insane," I continued to protest. "Look at me"—I gestured up and down—"I have one power that I've *slightly* perfected. I know of fantasy, supernatural, and paranormal world issues only because of a shit ton of reading books. I am no one of power, no one to be leading, no one to be making decisions."

Rhône pursed their lips. "Then you have advisors. You use that fabulous open heart and intelligent brain to learn absolutely everything you can about your position, your powers, and the issues our community faces. You show them your honesty, your openness, your ability to accept, and your unique perspective. You earn their respect, their trust, and their admiration." Rhône kissed me softly, the sweet taste of popid tea still lingering on their lips. "This is going to happen."

"But I'm not ready. I don't think it's a good idea."

"Whether you're ready or not, it's going to happen." Rhône pulled me in for a hug.

"I can't do it without you by my side," I whispered, still not ready to believe all that Rhône had told me.

"There's nowhere I'd rather be." Rhône buried their face in my neck. "My entire life, I've known I was one of the most powerful of my people. But I always felt that something was missing." They looked up with tears in their eyes. "And then I met you, and it's like all of the missing pieces clicked. We were born to lead, Kel. Born to be together. You're as much a part of me as I am of you. You are my destiny."

"And you're mine," I murmured.

"Let's get back to the ceremony." Rhône nuzzled their nose along my jaw before kissing me softly.

I spent the next hour or so with Rhône, dancing, laughing, rejoicing in our blessings and throwing every bit of positivity to our Mother Earth.

THE NEXT MORNING, I woke with Rhône in my arms. "I want to wake up like this every day for the rest of my life."

"That can probably be arranged," Rhône mumbled into my chest.

"When will Ximon be allowed to return to the popids?"

Rhône was silent for a beat before answering. "Within a few days most likely. Why?"

"I think I'd like to have final words with zir." The thought of talking to one of my biological parents one last time had been pestering me for a bit. "I feel like I'll regret it if I don't."

Rhône nodded. "I can understand that. The last time you spoke to Ximon, you didn't realize you were speaking to your own flesh and blood."

"Yet Ximon knew I'm their son," I murmured. "Part of me would like to think that's why they asked to speak to me."

"Perhaps. I'm sure there are parts of the past that Ximon regrets."

"Let's eat breakfast, and then I'll ask your parents if I may see Ximon."

Rhône nodded and stretched before climbing from bed. "Do you want me with you?"

"I always want you with me," I whispered and kissed their cheek.

Rhône smiled. "Then we're on the same page."

After breakfast, I asked Nayel and Rube if I could have some last words with Ximon.

"I think that is a very wise," Nayel stated.

"Yes, speaking to Ximon now that you know they are your biological father will likely provide a lot of closure for you." Rube patted my arm.

Rhône and I walked to the area of the village where Ximon was being held.

"Thank you for your service. You may take a break." Rhône spoke to the Popids who had been keeping Ximon's powers at bay. "I will protect Kellan and keep Ximon's powers neutralized."

The Popids nodded and left the three of us alone.

"Not to worry, I have no more reasons to use my powers against the village," Ximon spoke quietly from their cell.

I pulled a chair close to the bars and sat.

"How may I help you, Kellan?"

"You're my father," I stated.

"Yes," Ximon nodded.

"You've known about me since my conception." It wasn't a question.

Ximon nodded.

"Why did you hide me? Why did you not want to know me?" My voice cracked with emotion I hadn't been prepared to feel.

Ximon ran a hand over their long white beard. "There are a variety of answers to the question of why I helped to keep you away from the extra-sapien community. But please don't ever think that I didn't want to know you. I watched you from afar. I felt as if I knew you as I watched you grow up."

Tears welled in my eyes. "I didn't know."

"If you had known, then my magic wasn't doing its job."

"Why did you hide me? Undermine the village?"

"Hiding you was Maris and Maeve's idea mostly. I helped with it as needed because I knew you'd one day be very powerful, much more powerful than me, and I didn't relish giving up my position." Ximon leaned both elbows on zir knees. "Sabotaging the village is not something I'm proud of and I do not wish to speak of it."

"I'm sad." I shifted in my chair. "Sad because you'd rather take a coward's way out than own your mistakes and be there for me. You're my *father*, yet I'll have to learn of my powers from others. You gave me life, you gave me the best *real* parents I could ever ask for, and for those things, I am grateful. I wish things could be different between us, wish we could form a relationship, but it appears you're too jaded and bitter to see the good anymore. I'm lucky that Nayel and Rube will teach me what you won't be around to teach."

Ximon was silent for a moment. "I'm not a good Popid. I'm not someone you should be associated with. You turned out to be an amazing individual, but I'm not responsible for that." Ximon reached a hand to touch mine, and I allowed it. "You were always better off with your outer world parents. You'll be much better with Nayel, Rube, and Rhône as your support and teachers."

I squeezed Ximon's hand. "If you're allowed to come back, for your second calling or whatever it's called, like a second chance..." I paused to collect my thoughts. "If you get that second chance, I hope you're able to take it and make things right. If it's within my lifetime, I'd like very much if you would look me up."

For the first time, Ximon seemed affected by my words. "I'd like that, too."

I let go of Ximon's hand and stood.

"Will you be at the returning?" Ximon asked.

I turned to Rhône.

They nodded.

I swallowed hard. "It appears I will be there." I had no clue what to expect at an event where a being was basically being allowed to die and pass on. Knowing it was my father being—was sacrificed even the right word?—made it even more difficult.

We left Ximon and walked toward the popid fields, hand-in-hand.

"Are you okay?" Rhône asked.

I sorted the words in my head for several minutes. When I reached the fields, I sat with Rhône on a bench and absorbed the power of the popids. I finally spoke, "I've got this whole jumble of feelings. On one hand, I'm angry at all the time stolen from me, and Ximon's part in that, but I also cherish my childhood and my *real* parents. I wouldn't have wanted to miss that. On the other hand, I'm sad that I'll never get to know my birth father, and most likely my birth mother, as well. But I don't like the type of people they turned out to be, so maybe I'm not missing out on much." I ran a hand over my face. "So, I'm kinda okay and kinda not, if that makes sense."

Rhône laid their head on my shoulder. "It's okay to not be okay."

"Well, then, I'm okay." I kissed the top of their head.

———

THE NEXT FEW days were fairly quiet in the village. The elders met to consider Ximon's request to return to the popids. After much deliberation, the request was approved. Ximon was the first Popid to make the request *and* be deemed fit to make that type of decision in several decades.

The day before the return service was packed full of preparations. I was shocked at how similar to a ceremony the service appeared to be. It was almost like a funeral. Shouldn't it be a sad occasion?

Rhône heard my thoughts. "While we are sad to lose Ximon, we also choose to focus on the positives and celebrate the life they had instead of mourning their loss. This was Ximon's request, a last wish if you will. We will honor that choice as well as honor the good that Ximon did."

"So, the wrongs will just be swept away?" I frowned.

"Somewhat," Rhône agreed. "But it's not really our place to hand down consequences after a Popid has asked to return to the flowers."

"I guess." It did make sense, overall. Ximon had made a final decision and would receive whatever punishment Mother Earth, the greater being, or whoever decided.

When the day of the return service arrived, I dressed in light, loose Popid clothing and joined in the ritual.

"What is bothering you?" Rhône asked.

I shrugged and smiled slightly. "Even now, it's so weird that you can do that." I gestured between our heads. "The reading my mind thing." I knotted the rope belt around my tunic. "I think what's been bothering me is that this seems almost like a sacrifice. Like Ximon is being sacrificed to Mother Earth. But if they requested this to be how their life ended, it's not really a sacrifice, is it? A sacrifice seems wrong, like against a person's will."

"I understand how it could feel like a sacrifice," Rhône agreed. "But you're right, Ximon chose this rather than stand trial for their wrongdoings, and Popid practice allows for any villager to make that request. Ximon was deemed mentally stable to make the request. They know they will face an eternity of limbo if they aren't called to make amends in a next life."

Voicing my concerns about the difference between *allowing* Ximon to return to the popids rather than forcefully sacrificing them seemed to help clear my head.

In the end, the entire village gathered around Ximon and said their farewells. Ximon was then led to the very center of the largest popid field by the elders along with myself and Rhône. The rest of the village sang songs of love and goodbyes while each elder said something kind to Ximon. Finally, it was Rhône's turn to speak to Ximon.

"Ximon, thank you for Kellan. You've made mistakes, but he is your greatest achievement, and that will live on for generations to come." Rhône kissed Ximon's cheek.

Knowing I was next, I cleared my throat. "Thank you for my life, my blood, my powers. I aspire to make you proud, but also to be better than you in every single way. Your descendants will know of your part in their existence." I hesitated, but took a step closer and pulled Ximon into a hug. "Godspeed," I whispered.

Ximon lay down in the popids and crossed their arms over their chest.

The rest of us chanted and sang our farewells as we left the field.

"What happens now?" I stared at the middle of the field where we had left Ximon.

"The popids will welcome Ximon back to the arms of Mother Earth."

I glanced at Rhône.

They shrugged. "We only know that within a week Ximon will be completely gone. The actual process is not one we are privy to. It's a somewhat vague transaction in my mind."

One by one the Popids returned to the village. I stood rooted to the spot, but Rhône took my hand and gently led me toward the dining hall where a large meal was served.

When the meal was drawing to an end, Fynn stood and declared an elder meeting was in order. "We've been given some information in regards to Maeve and Maris Winston."

I glanced at Rhône, eyes wide. "You think they'll tell us what happened?"

Rhône winked, but shrugged as they watched Nayel and Rube approach.

"Kellan and Rhône, your presence is requested at

this meeting," Nayel's deep voice gave importance to the words.

I gaped, but stood and followed the elders to Elder Hall.

Fynn started the meeting. "News has been delivered to us regarding Maeve and Maris. We will share it within the committee first and then allow the details to be passed on to the village. Nayel, please impart the information."

Nayel stood and cleared their throat. "The Popids submitted our reports to the outer world government, the DPSFS board of directors, and the top members of the extra-sapien community. We did note that Maeve and Maris had been cooperative in our questioning." Nayel thumbed through some pages. "Dr. Maeve Winston has been removed from her position at the DPSFS and banned from anything related to that department. She has also been arrested by the extra-sapien enforcement agency for behavior unbecoming of a top extra-sapien official." They flipped to another page. "Maris Winston has been cited by the outer world government for hiding her extra-sapien blood and being involved with a Popid, which is deemed behavior unbecoming of a government official. She's also been arrested by the extra-sapien enforcement agency for unbecoming behavior, misuse of her position, and taking advantage of her sister's power and prestige."

I took in the information, attempting to allow my

brain time to process. "So, what happens to them now?"

Nayel turned another page. "Maeve and Maris will be sent to a desolate forest area of the farthest outer ring. They will be allowed to keep their magic in hopes of survival, but they can never return to the extra-sapien community. They are officially banished until the end of time or their deaths, whichever comes first."

My mouth dropped open. "For real?" *Whoa, that was some serious punishment.*

"For what they did to you, I'm surprised they get to keep their powers," Rube stated.

I could only shake my head. "I should feel sad for them. But they sabotaged so much of my life, they misused their powers and positions, and so, I have a hard time feeling bad."

"Completely understandable." Rube nodded.

"There's another order of business." Nayel shuffled papers as they spoke. "Kellan, this isn't something I've spoken to you about yet, but I'd like to nominate Kellan and Rhône for a position on the elder committee."

I sucked in a breath and shook my head. "No, that's not even possible."

Nayel held up a hand. "You and Rhône would act as one person, and the nomination would be provisional. Rhône was already slated for nomination. Now the two of you will serve on the board as one. You'll learn from Rhône and eventually earn your own spot."

"Why not just nominate Rhône and then nominate me in the future *if* I prove qualified?"

Rube smiled. "Such a hardheaded young man." They shook their head. "Kellan, you are flesh and blood of one of the most powerful Popids to ever exist *and* the twin sister of Dr. Maeve Winston. Your powers are deeply ingrained and will only grow and improve with time, support, and practice. You don't need to *prove* yourself. Your birth is proof enough."

"Let's vote on the nomination," Nayel called.

The entire committee voted yes.

Holy shit.

———

THE CALL from DPSFS came the next day.

Rhône and I left the village at the request of the department and made our way to a one-o'clock meeting with the DPSFS board of directors.

"I'm sure they just want to check that all is okay after what Maeve did. Not like I'd sue or anything. Maybe they'll finally approve my application, you think?" I chatted nonstop as we walked up the steps of the large stone building.

Rhône simply laughed and shook their head. "I'm pretty sure you're a shoo-in now."

By the time I stood at the exit of the DPSFS, I was in complete disbelief.

The president of the board of directors shook my

hand. "We've given you a lot to think about, Kellan. Take your time, but we'd like an answer in a week's time if possible."

I could only nod.

Rhône took my hand. "Just give it some time to process. Do you want to do anything while we're away from the village?"

I stared at them for a few seconds. "I need to see my parents. Will you come with me?"

"There's never a time I won't stand by your side," Rhône assured. "Yes, of course."

———

I TOOK the steps to my parents' house two at a time and pulled Rhône close to my side when we reached the door. "I've never really introduced anyone to my parents, like not anyone more than a friend."

Rhône crinkled their nose. "I don't have to go in. I can meet you back at the village."

"What? No!" I kissed their lips. "That's not what I meant. Just that this is a first for me, and I'm nervous. So"—I gestured toward the door—"if I act like an idiot, just cut me some slack."

Rhône barked out a laugh. "I'll keep that in mind." Zie leaned in and nuzzled my neck. "If it's any consolation, I most definitely have never been introduced to a lover's family."

I took a deep breath. "Day of firsts then. Actually,

it's been several days of firsts and learning new things. I'm afraid my brain and heart can't take much more." Dropping a kiss on Rhône's nose, I knocked at the door.

My mother answered the door and immediately broke into the most gorgeous, welcoming smile and pulled me into a hug. "Kellan! Oh, what a surprise. Come in, come in."

I felt the moment Mom realized I wasn't alone.

"Oh, goodness me. Where are my manners?" Mom pushed me aside and stepped in front of Rhône. "My name is Marian. Are you Rhône?" She turned to me and touched my cheek. "They are even more beautiful than you described." Then Mom spoke again to Rhône. "I'm so very happy to meet you. Kellan has never brought a date or anything like that home to meet us. This is most definitely a special occasion."

My cheeks grew hot, and I ran a hand over my face.

Rhône simply grinned from ear to ear and let my mom gush over them.

We followed Mom into the house as she yelled for my dad. "Louis! Louis, get in here. Kellan came to visit and brought his *friend* Rhône."

I kinda love your mom already. Rhône winked at me.

Don't encourage her. She'll have you looking at baby pictures and drinking pathetic tea all too soon. I shook my head.

Rhône laughed. *Can't wait.*

Dad came around the corner and removed his reading glasses before glancing at Rhône and me.

For one brief moment, I was fearful of his reaction.

But then Dad smiled and my heart remembered how good these people were.

"Kellan, son, so good to see you." Dad clapped me on the back before pulling me into a hug. "Now, introduce me to your friend." He was all smiles as he turned to Rhône.

"Louis, this is Rhône. Remember, I told you about *them?*"

My eyes grew wide, and I shot a look at Rhône, but they were smiling and letting Dad pull them into a hug.

"Rhône, yes, now I remember." Dad maneuvered himself so he had Rhône on one side and me on the other. "What a special day! How long can you two stay?"

"Oh, you'll stay for dinner, yes?" Mom clasped her hands at her chest. "Nothing fancy, but we'd love to have you."

I glanced around Dad to catch Rhône's eye. They nodded and smiled.

"Sure, we can stay."

That began an hour of Dad showing us his little garden out back.

"My tomatoes should be absolute beauties this year," Dad spoke proudly as he rubbed the leaf of a small tomato plant.

Maybe we should hook him up with some popid fertilizer. Rhône waggled their brows.

I snorted and covered it with a cough.

"Y'all come in," Mom hollered out the back door. "Dinner is ready."

I winced when I saw what was for dinner. I absolutely adored chipped beef on toast, but I'd heard enough complaints about "shit on a shingle" throughout my life to know it wasn't something everyone loved.

If you don't like what we're having, we can eat back at the village. I pulled out a chair for Rhône.

Nonsense, it smells amazing. I'm excited to try it.

My heart clenched, and my stomach fluttered at how much I loved them.

"Like I said, not fancy." Mom sounded apologetic. "But I'd like to think it's the best chipped beef on toast you'll ever taste." She passed the plate of toast to Rhône before ladling out the salted beef gravy onto her own plate.

Rhône took two pieces of toast just like Mom had done. "It smells delicious. I've never had this meal before, I'm very excited to try it." They then copied Mom's actions and ladled gravy directly onto their toast.

"Never had chipped beef on toast?" Dad asked, eyes wide. "Ever heard of *shit on a shingle?*"

Rhône snorted. "Can't say that I have."

Once everyone had their plates ready, Mom asked Dad to say grace.

"Father, thank you for the blessings you've provided and for the food before us and for the wonderful surprise of having Kellan and Rhône with us today. Amen." Dad ended the prayer and glanced at Rhône. "I know organized religion earned itself a bad name, but we still feel it's important to offer our gratitude toward our maker."

"Agreed," Rhône said with a smile.

I took a big bite of toast and gravy and chewed while I watched Rhône do the same.

They chewed their bite, and a huge smile filled their face. "This is amazing," they exclaimed. "I have to get the recipe so we can have it in the village." Immediately, Rhône clamped their mouth shut and looked guilty. *I'm so sorry.*

No worries.

Mom and Dad gave Rhône and me curious looks, but we all continued with the delicious meal.

"Louis and Kellan will do the dishes," Mom told Rhône. "You and I can look through some of Kellan's old baby pictures."

I groaned, but Rhône laughed.

"That sounds like a fabulous idea, Mrs. Roberts."

"Oh dear, no, call me Marian." Mom swept Rhône from the room, leaving Dad and me to clean up.

"Rhône seems very nice," Dad offered as he carried plates to the sink.

"They're the best, truly. Never felt this way about anyone in my life." I wiped down the table.

"That's good to hear." Dad nodded and added soap to the dishwater. "Your mom and I just want you safe, happy, and healthy. That's all we've ever wanted for you."

"I am," I stated, more sure of my words than any I'd ever spoken.

"Well, we should finish up in here before your mom gets through all the best pictures." Dad snapped me with a dishtowel.

"Ouch!" I laughed.

"The towel or the pictures?"

"Both," I grumbled.

An hour later, Mom had gone through all of the photo albums, and I was thoroughly embarrassed.

Stop. You were an adorable baby and child. Your awkward teen years didn't seem as bad as some of the stories I've read or heard.

I snorted.

Are you going to ask them about your adoption?

I sighed. I knew I needed to. *They're so happy. I don't want to upset them.*

You do what you think is best. I'll support you no matter what.

I took a deep breath. "Mom, Dad, I want to ask you something."

"Of course, anything," Mom answered.

"Did you know anything about my birth parents?" I blurted. Smooth.

Mom gasped and turned teary eyes to my dad. She held a trembling hand to her mouth, and Dad put his arm around her. "Oh Kellan, I'm so sorry." Her words wavered as she wiped her eyes. "I always wanted to tell you, but we were made to sign papers that swore we'd never look for your parents or tell you about the adoption."

"No, Mom, I'm not angry. I just wondered if you knew my birth parents."

"No, we were told nothing." Dad's words were gruff as he pulled Mom closer to his side and kissed the side of her head. "We'd wanted a child forever. When the adoption agency said they had a newborn, we were so over the moon that we didn't ask many questions. Just signed the papers saying we'd keep your adoption a secret and never look for your parents."

I nodded. I'd figured as much.

"I'd like to think we did all right by you," Dad hedged.

"You guys are my only *real* parents. Period."

"You raised the most amazing, caring, intelligent, loving person I've ever had the pleasure of knowing," Rhône interjected.

Heat crept up my neck and blossomed on my cheeks.

"That's a beautiful thing to say," Mom whispered. She turned and patted my hand. "How did you find out?" Then with a look of fear she said, "Oh dear, do you think we'll be in violation of those papers we signed?"

"No, you guys won't be in any trouble," I assured. "So, I'm going to tell you some things that may be a little hard to believe. I won't overwhelm you with it all at once, and we'll take our time. But please know that I speak the truth, even if it's outside of what you've known and believed before."

I spent the next hour giving Mom and Dad bits and pieces of information, not wanting to overwhelm them. I told them of the Popid village and finding out about my birth parents, but I left out a lot. *I'll share a bit each time I see them.* I glanced at Rhône, and they nodded.

By the time I'd finished, Mom and Dad looked a bit shell shocked, but they attempted to take it all in stride.

"Well, I'd sure like to see these popoid fields you're talking about," Dad stated.

"Popid," I corrected. "I'm thinking we could make that happen." I gave Rhône a sideways glance.

"Of course, we can. My parents would love to host Kellan's parents for dinner one evening. They've become quite fond of your son," Rhône explained.

"That's so very kind," Mom murmured.

"We should probably be heading out." I stood and held out my hand for Rhône. "I'd like to make these visits a once-a-week thing. Would you guys be okay with that?"

"Dinner with you and Rhône once a week? That would be absolutely fantastic," Mom gushed.

We all exchanged hugs and pleasant farewells before Rhône and I walked into the dark night.

"Could I possibly love them anymore?" Rhône asked. "I can see why you turned out so amazing."

I started to protest, but then I realized that Rhône was right. My parents, Louis and Marian Roberts, my *real* parents, were exactly the reason I turned out to be a good person. "They *are* amazing."

———

THE VILLAGE WAS CALM, quiet, and peaceful when we arrived. We said a few hellos and made small-talk with a couple villagers as we made our way to our room.

"Do you think any of the villagers are jealous or mad about me just waltzing in here and becoming part of your world? I mean, they voted me to the elder board. That's something that some Popids work for their entire life." I sat on the edge of the bed and patted the mattress for Rhône to join me.

They thought about my question for several moments. "No, I don't think so. The very core of our existence is to focus on and celebrate the positives in our lives and in our world. It would go against all that we are to feel negatively toward someone so very good coming into our village."

Rhône's words made sense, but I still considered myself an outsider.

"Well, get over that," Rhône quipped. "You are a Popid elder. You're sort of like royalty here now. If the Popids didn't already love you, they do now."

I shook my head. "It's just so much to take in. I never want to become as jaded as Ximon or as deceitful and angry as Maeve and Maris." I pulled Rhône close to me. "Promise me. Promise we'll always stand together and stand for what is right."

Rhône tucked their head into my chest. "Always."

"I feel like I could sleep for days," I murmured. "Shower?"

We spent thirty minutes in an amazing hot shower. I swore Popid water had special properties.

"It does." Rhône's hands roamed my body. "But I think sharing the water with you has just as many special properties."

We kissed, touched, and stroked until we were both trembling. As we came apart in each other's arms, I held Rhône close and pledged my forever love.

Once dried and dressed in sparse clothing, I thumbed through my phone and chose a song.

When it began to play, Rhône turned to me with a smile. "What's this for?"

I held out my hand. "May I have this dance?"

I vowed then and there that I would spend the rest of my life putting that smile on Rhône's face.

Three songs later, Rhône and I fell into bed. I once again took Rhône's long, thick shaft in my hand and stroked. "I want this. I want you, please, Rhône." I leaned down and licked the head.

Rhône rolled me to my back and slicked their fingers before teasing my hole.

"I don't need to be prepped. I want to feel the sting."

Rhône moved to press gently into my body. When they were inside me fully, I rocked my hips, trying to make them move.

"No, this is going to be slow and gentle," Rhône whispered. They thrust in and out of my body in the most agonizingly slow motion as zie stroked my throbbing cock.

When I exploded hot and thick between us, Rhône captured my lips in a kiss and emptied themselves into my ass.

Several moments later, we'd cleaned up and crawled back into bed.

"Tell me your thoughts," Rhône whispered.

"If I don't, you'll know them anyway," I teased.

"Yes, but I like hearing them in your words."

"I'm scared." I rolled to face Rhône. "So much has changed so fast."

"That's understandable."

"But I'm also so very excited to begin this journey. It's like some bad stuff had to happen in order for the good to be discovered. And I'm scared, but all my lifelong dreams are coming true." I reached out and stroked Rhône's hair. "All I ever wanted was to be part of something extra-sapien."

"And now you're not just *part of* something extra-sapien; you're one of the most powerful extra-sapiens in the community." Rhône ran a hand down my arm and laced our fingers together.

"Well, it's a lot of untapped power right now," I mumbled.

"We'll have you in tip-top shape in no time," Rhône promised.

"There's something else, though," I said.

Rhône raised zir brows.

"I won't do any of this without you by my side."

"Kellan, you are powerful on your own," Rhône began.

I interrupted. "I'm not saying I *can't* do it without you. I'm saying I *won't* do it without you. Nothing in my life felt complete until I met you. After you, everything made sense and fell into place. I require you by my side for everything that is to come."

"Require?" Rhône smirked. "Power position already going to your head?" They tickled me.

I laughed and rolled on top of Rhône. "No tickling!"

"So, let me get this straight. You *require* me by your side, you're heading into a powerful and lofty position, yet you surrender to tickling?" Rhône teased and threatened with tickly fingers.

"Okay, how about this? I *request* you to be by my side through this journey. And we keep the ticklish thing a secret between just us?" I caught their hands and pinned them down. "I can't be taking positions of power and worry my adversaries might learn of my ticklish weakness." I leaned down close, Rhône's hands still pinned, and kissed them deeply on the mouth. "Please? Stand by my side? And keep my secret?"

"I will *forever* stand by you and support you. We are one in power, in position, in love." Rhône kissed me back. "But it's always nice to hear you beg," they teased.

"You're the only person I want to spend the rest of my life begging," I whispered as I wrapped Rhône in my arms and pulled the blanket over our bodies.

EPILOGUE

"MR. ROBERTS, we're so glad you've accepted our offer to head the DPSFS," one of the head honchos spoke as he opened the door to Maeve Winston's old office.

"Co-head," I reminded them. "And please, it's Kellan. Rhône and I are excited to take on this challenge."

"Yes, of course," the man agreed. "It's highly unusual for a Popid to be in such a high position in the DPSFS. And having co-heads of the department is unheard of."

I raised my brows wondering if the board of directors had changed their mind.

"But after what we learned of you from Dr. Winston, her sister, and from the Popid village, we couldn't *not* have you here leading us. And if you request Popid Rhône to share the position, we can only trust your wisdom."

"Thank you." I ran my hand over the desk. All evidence of Maeve was gone, but I felt like an intruder in her former office.

"Is there anything else I can do for you, Kellan? Rhône?"

I shook my head. "No, thank you. We'll call you if needed. I'd like to set up the office and perhaps get some meetings scheduled. You'll have the extra desk and chair delivered soon?"

"Yes, yes, of course," the man assured. "Then I'll leave you two to settle in."

And then Rhône and I were alone.

"I sat at this desk more than once, trusting Maeve and learning of your world," I murmured. "Oh, how the mighty have fallen."

"Oh, how the mighty are rising," Rhône quipped.

After speaking to Nayel, Rube, and Rhône, we'd decided that I would take the DPSFS offer to replace Dr. Winston. Having Rhône share the position was my one demand.

We planned to spend two to three days a week at the department. We also planned to open up the department, bring more transparency to the DPSFS and the extra-sapien community at large. No more opportunities for leaders to hide their wrong-doings. I didn't want to rule the department as Maeve had. I wanted to be open, welcome, and *honest* from the very beginning.

I sat in the fancy chair and spun around several

times before my eyes caught on the wall safe, and I brought the chair to a screeching halt.

"We need him back. We need the key to that safe."

Rhône laughed and stared at me.

"Oh, right," I mumbled. "Sorry, it's going to take forever to get used to my magic powers."

"It's not all *magic* per se," Rhône reminded.

"Can you help me?" I walked to the safe and reached out my hand for Rhône.

"Focus on what you want to do," Rhône guided. "Talk it through."

"I want the safe to open." I stared at the lock. Plucking the muscovite crystal from my pocket, I held it over the lock, closed my eyes, and imagined the lock opening.

When I heard the click, I opened my eyes to find Rhône beaming at me. "You are learning things so quickly. I'm so proud of you."

I pulled the safe door open and found two envelopes. I took them out and returned to the desk, leaning on the edge. The smaller envelope was the one Maeve had me sign. The larger envelope also had my name on it.

My hands trembled somewhat as I opened the letter I had signed.

Kellan,

Your powers are beyond anything I've ever seen or experienced. When you've learned to use them, you will be a force no one will want to reckon with. I'm sorry for my part in this mess.

Maeve

I wasn't sure what I'd expected. She had only written for a few moments before asking me to sign the envelope. She'd known, that very first day, Maeve had *known* me and what had been done to me. Maybe that's why she was so kind and helpful, maybe it was her way of trying to make up for her wrongs.

I slid a finger under the flap of the second envelope.

This letter was addressed to me and was dated the day Maeve was arrested.

Dear Kellan,

There are no words to adequately apologize for what I did to you, but I am sorry. I was wrong to deceive and lie, but I was also foolish to think a power like yours could ever be hidden. I let my jilted, angry, selfish heart rule me, and that was wrong.

Your powers are not the only thing special about you. From the moment I met you, I was floored by your open heart, your accepting soul, your intelligence, and your ability to love despite differences. Powers or no, these qualities make you an exceptional young man, and I'm sorry I won't be around to see you prosper and succeed. I would like to think I would have been a good Aunt Maeve if I hadn't messed things up so thoroughly.

Hone your powers, learn all that you can, be a great leader, but don't ever stop being the kindhearted, open, accepting person you've always been. Learn from me; don't let a selfish soul guide you. Stand for what is right. Always.

I wish I had a chance to do things differently.

Take care,

Maeve

"Wow," I breathed out. "Is it possible to hate her yet love her all the same?"

"I believe so," Rhône murmured. "And she's right."

"About?"

"Part of why you'll be an outstanding leader is because you're open and accepting, and you stand for what is right. You are so very smart, and you love fiercely despite differences." Rhône wrapped their arms around me.

I stood and held Rhône close as I gazed around the office. *Our* office. "I want to use my human background in tandem with my extra-sapien blood to affect change." My heart swelled with purpose and hope. "Different isn't bad. Differences shouldn't separate us. Differences should be celebrated and respected."

"I think you just came up with our DPSFS mission statement." Rhône chuckled.

"We'll get it on our letterhead," I teased.

"This is going to be good. Really good," Rhône promised.

"Yeah, I think you're right." I nodded and smiled as we faced the beginning of this journey.

A NOTE FROM THE AUTHOR

Rhône is a genderqueer, intersex individual who uses gender neutral pronouns in this story. Rhône prefers they/them and zie/zir. They/them and zie/zir are used interchangeably in this story. Zie replaces he/she and zir replaces him/her. The author links to more information on gender neutral pronouns later in this note.

A note on intersex:

Information about real-world intersex individuals can be found at The Intersex Society of North America. http://www.isna.org/faq/what_is_intersex

One of the fictional parts of this story and where the author took liberties is that Popids have completely functioning male and female sex organs and systems, and that they aren't subject to gender assignment surgeries as non-consenting infants and/or hormones trying to force their body to act a certain way.

Quoted from http://www.isna.org "The Intersex Society of North America (ISNA) is devoted to systemic change to end shame, secrecy, and unwanted genital surgeries for people born with an anatomy that someone decided is not standard for male or female.

We have learned from listening to individuals and families dealing with intersex that:

- Intersexuality is primarily a problem of stigma and trauma, not gender.
- Parents' distress must not be treated by surgery on the child.
- Professional mental health care is essential.
- Honest, complete disclosure is good medicine.
- All children should be assigned as boy or girl, without early surgery."

A note on intersectionality:

Kellan and Rhône (like so many of us) have a great deal of intersectionality.

**   https://www.dictionary.com/browse/intersectionality

**   https://www.ywboston.org/2017/03/what-is-intersectionality-and-what-does-it-have-to-do-with-me/

A note on gender neutral pronouns:

The author used they/them and zie/zir pronouns for

Rhône and other Popids. There are several other gender-neutral pronouns. Read more here: https://uwm.edu/lgbtrc/support/gender-pronouns/

Also, the use of singular they is becoming (and should become) more used and accepted.

    ** https://public.oed.com/blog/a-brief-history-of-singular-they/

    ** https://www.grammarly.com/blog/use-the-singular-they/

    ** https://aceseditors.org/news/2017/ap-style-for-first-time-allows-use-of-they-as-singular-pronoun/

A note on gender-related terms:

A glossary of gender-related terms-

    *https://www.hrc.org/resources/glossary-of-terms

    *https://www.glaad.org/reference/lgbtq

    *https://www.glaad.org/reference/transgender

Some other words it may be helpful to know:

- *Enby- In the LGBTQ community, an enby is a nonbinary person. It's a phonetic pronunciation of NB, short for nonbinary, or people who do not identify their gender as male or female.*
- *Non-binary- An adjective describing a person who does not identify exclusively as a man or a woman. Non-binary people may identify as being both a man*

and a woman, somewhere in between, or as falling completely outside these categories. While many also identify as transgender, not all non-binary people do.

- *Pansexual-* Describes someone who has the potential for emotional, romantic or sexual attraction to people of any gender though not necessarily simultaneously, in the same way or to the same degree.

- *Gender non-conforming* - A broad term referring to people who do not behave in a way that conforms to the traditional expectations of their gender, or whose gender expression does not fit neatly into a category.

- *Genderqueer* - Genderqueer people typically reject notions of static categories of gender and embrace a fluidity of gender identity and often, though not always, sexual orientation. People who identify as "genderqueer" may see themselves as being both male and female, neither male nor female or as falling completely outside these categories.

ACKNOWLEDGMENTS

It's always so hard to write this part because I'm worried I'll forget someone without meaning to.

Readers- you are the reason I write. As long as you continue reading my stories, I'll continue writing them. Thank you for your support.

Bloggers- your support, reviews, and promotion are very much appreciated. Thank you!

My author buddies- I don't know that I could keep doing this without our brainstorm sessions, laughter, road trips, meals, wine, and friendship as my support.

Thank you to my betas, editors, proofreaders, and ARC readers! Your eyes and input are beyond important to me.

Brett and Gage- as usual, I doubt you even grasp how much your support, input, and friendship mean to me. This author journey had brought many wonderful things into my life, and you both are two of the BEST! I'm blessed to call you friends.

My family and friends- thank you for your love and support, always.

ABOUT THE AUTHOR

A.D. Ellis is an Indiana girl, born and raised. She spends much of her time in central Indiana as an instructional coach/teacher in the inner city of Indianapolis, being a mom to two amazing school-aged children, and wondering how she and her husband of almost two decades have managed to not drive each other insane. A lot of her time is also devoted to phone call avoidance and her hatred of cooking.

She loves chocolate, wine, pizza, and naps along with reading and writing romance. These loves don't leave much time for housework, much to the chagrin of her husband. Who would pick cleaning the house over a nap or a good book? She uses any extra time to increase her fluency in sarcasm.

Find all of Ellis' contemporary romance and male/male romance at www.adellisauthor.com

FREE books-- sign up at bit.ly/ADEllisNews for a FREE male/female romance.

Sign up at http://www.subscribepage.com/ADEllisNewsMMRomance for a FREE male/male romance book.

ALSO BY A.D. ELLIS

The BJ Boys Series (3 books)

Something About Him Series (6 books)

His Reluctant Cowboy

————

Plus several other titles:

The Storm's Gift

Holiday Island

Devoted (a Something About Him novella)

Saving Us

Stranded Hearts (a short story)

Eli & Gage (a Something About Him short story)

————

A.D.'s first stories (all male/female except Sawyer which is male/male) are in the Torey Hope and Torey Hope: The Later Years series. Find the 8 book box set on Amazon.